MW01093568

THE THING I DIDN'T KNOW I DIDN'T KNOW

BRENT HARTINGER

BOOKS

BK Books
www.brenthartinger.com

Cover design by Philip Malaczewski

ISBN-13: 978-0-9846794-8-5

For Michael Jensen

And for everyone in the twenties
Spoiler alert! Life all works out in the end

CHAPTER ONE

So I was officially lost. And it was well after dark in a bad part of town.

Is it okay to say that—a "bad" part of town? Because I know there are people who are sensitive to that kind of talk. But the fact is, the garbage cans were overflowing, and the air smelled of beer, piss, and, well, trash from the garbage cans. The Korean grocery on my right was the kind that seals up with a big metal grate, so tight that you can't tell if they're permanently out of business or just closed for the night. In front of me, something black darted across the sidewalk—either a small cat or a *huge* rat. A minute earlier, there'd been cars passing by, but suddenly the street next to the sidewalk was empty.

Screw it, I'm making an actual value judgment: this was a part of Seattle I did *not* want to be in. How far had I walked, anyway? Was I even on the right street? Somehow I'd become disoriented in the dark.

Halfway down the block, I passed an alley. There was someone just inside, not five feet away, staring out at me. He was wearing a hoodie, so I couldn't see his face, but I could tell he was young, maybe a teenager. I jerked back, surprised, but the guy stayed where he was, like an actor in a haunted house who'd been given specific instructions about exactly how far he could go.

"Whachu lookin' for?" he said.

"Huh?" I said, even as I realized he was talking about drugs. "Nothing. A friend."

I hurried forward, but that's when I discovered the first guy hadn't been alone, that the street wasn't as deserted as I'd thought. There were two guys sitting on the stoop in a recessed doorway across the street, their faces somehow perfectly obscured by the shadows. And the blinds moved in the window of an apartment above—someone was looking down at me, but the face was hidden behind reflections in the glass.

They were watching me, all these figures in the dark. But one way or another, I couldn't make out any of their faces. Why was this street so dark anyway? Had someone shot out the streetlights?

My name is Russel Middlebrook, and I'm twenty-three years old. And if this all reads like "privileged middle class white boy goes into the city at night and gets freaked out by all the poor people," well, yeah, there's probably some truth to that. But that still doesn't mean it wasn't scary.

Back in high school, whenever I was in an uncomfortable situation, I had this habit of imagining that things were much worse than they were. So if, say, I was anxious in the locker room after gym class, worried that someone would call me a fag, I'd imagine

I was a soldier on some bombed-out battlefield, lost behind enemy lines. Or if I was being hassled by jocks in the hallway, I'd imagine the whole school burning down around me. Looking back, I can see this must have been some sort of coping mechanism. It demystified the situation, reminded me that things could be a lot worse than they already were. Or maybe I was unconsciously trying to knock myself out of whatever funk I was in by making an ironic joke.

But I can't remember the last time I did that. I'm not sure why I stopped. Maybe it was because things now are usually already plenty scary, like here, on this depressing street in a bad part of town. (On the other hand, let's not romanticize the past too much, shall we? The high school locker room after gym class could be pretty fucking treacherous.)

A pigeon fluttered nearby, and I smelled something even fouler than before—hopefully a dead bird or dog, not a human corpse rotting away behind the broken windows of some forgotten basement.

I could still go back the way I'd come—the bus stop was only a couple of blocks back. But I'd already come this far. I figured I might as well see it through. So I walked onward, faster than before.

I reached the intersection at last, where there were streetlights and street signs again. I wasn't as lost as I'd thought. I could even see the address of the apartment building I was looking for. It was a grand old structure made of stone, like a monument to some dead president. But it'd be a president no one cared about anymore, because the stone was drab, and the windows were cluttered with knickknacks and awkwardly balanced air conditioners.

I crossed the street, trudged up the steps, and buzzed one of the apartments.

"Yeah?" said a voice from the speaker.

"It's me," I said. "Russel."

"I'll be right down."

Was the buzzer broken, or did he want to see me before actually letting me in? I didn't know, but I waited a minute or so until a figure trotted down the marble steps inside.

The light in the lobby was dim, so I couldn't get a good look at his face. He was wearing black running shorts and a green t-shirt. His skin was dark, olive— Latino or maybe Italian. And he didn't look much taller than I was, but he was broader, more solid. He walked with a confidence I couldn't even fake.

He stepped into the light just inside the door, and I could make out a face at last—the close-cropped hair, the pointed sideburns, the impossibly dark eyes. He was definitely handsome, even better-looking than his picture.

I let myself relax. But I didn't relax too much. There was still the actual matter of why I was meeting this guy in the first place—what came next. Even now, he was staring out at me like I was a fresh plump salmon on ice at the Pike Place Market.

Finally, he gave me a hungry smile and pushed the door open. I guess I'd passed the salmon inspection.

"I'm Boston," he said, and I nodded. That was the name of the guy I'd come to meet. "This way," he said, and he turned and led me back to the stairs.

Okay, so this is embarrassing. If you haven't figured it out by now, this was a hook-up. As in, for sex. An hour or so earlier, I'd been at home in my bedroom, chatting with this guy on this dating app. And before too long, he'd typed, *U lookn?*

And I hadn't said no. I mean, aren't we all looking for something? Peace, love, and understanding at least? I definitely was. But at that particular moment, even if I hadn't really wanted to admit it to myself, what I'd been looking for was sex. Simple, uncomplicated sex. Which isn't to say I'd done stuff like this very often before. Just two other times.

But one text had led to another, and he'd asked me if I wanted to come over to his place. It wasn't until I'd reached his neighborhood that I realized what that part of the city was like at night.

His apartment was small, one bedroom, and it smelled like dust and old kitchen grease. But at least the furniture was from Ikea, not Goodwill. The lights were off, but he'd left the TV on with the sound down low. It was some motocross show—the images flickered fast, almost like a strobe light.

The second the front door was closed, Boston stepped closer, facing me, standing with his feet wide apart. Then he leaned in, kissing me hard. I'd *definitely* passed the Pike Place Market inspection. But in fairness to Boston, I was kissing him back just as hard, which meant he'd passed my own salmon inspection. He tasted young and fresh and alive, the opposite of the smells on the street below, or even the apartment itself. There was a hint of something sweet—cola.

And then my hands were on him, fumbling, eager. He was a stone monument too, almost as hard as the apartment building, but alive, warm, pulsing under my fingers, covered with a layer of fine black hair. His hands were on me too, but not fumbling—his touch was as confident as his stride had been. We'd only exchanged a handful of words—and if you include the words we'd traded on that dating app, most of his had been misspelled. And yet here we were, alone, lips pressed together, teeth knocking, tongues touching, and fingers slipping past buttons and zippers and elastic, on a desperate, frenzied search to find, release, and explore whatever was sweaty and throbbing underneath.

An hour later, I was back home again, in the houseboat on Lake Union that I share with my friends Gunnar and Min.

Yeah, I live in Seattle on a houseboat. I know that's like saying, "I live in Ireland in a castle." Or, "I live in Alaska in an igloo." Living in a houseboat is just so "Seattle." To judge by the movies, you'd think we all live in houseboats. But the truth is there are only about five hundred of them on the whole lake. Which is a lot of houseboats compared to other cities, but still. And of course they're really expensive.

So how am I able to afford it at age twenty-three? It's actually my friend Gunnar's boat. When Gunnar was a senior in high school, he created this iPhone app called *Singing Dog*. It emits this high-pitched frequency that people (mostly) can't hear, but dogs can, causing them to bark out the tune of "I'm a Yankee Doodle Dandy" (sort of). The app doesn't work with every dog, but it works often enough that it went viral, and Gunnar ended up making something like nine hundred and fifty thousand dollars. In Gunnar's defense, he went to college anyway, and even applied himself. But mid-way through school, he took about four hundred thousand dollars and bought the house-boat, which is on the east side of Lake Union, halfway between school and downtown.

YOLO and all that, right?

On one hand, it was hard not to be jealous. After buying the houseboat, and taxes, and even student loans, he still had about two hundred thousand dollars left. Which means he didn't have to get a job, at least for the time being. On the other hand, he immediately invited my friend Min and me to live with him. He wouldn't even have charged us rent except that Min had insisted (and yes, I'd wanted to strangle her, even if I'd known she was right, that we'd be taking advantage of him otherwise). But at four hundred dollars a month, it's still a ridiculously sweet deal.

The houseboat isn't big, but it does have three bedrooms (although mine is more of a sleeping loft) and a really cool roof-top deck. It also has a small front room, which is where I found Gunnar and Min. They weren't ignoring each other exactly, but they were both on their tablets. That's the thing about liv-ing in a houseboat: As cool and "Seattle" as it all is, you end up spending a lot of time breathing down your roommates' necks.

"Hey, there," I said. Every now and then, the boat rocks a little on the water, or something sloshes, and it's exactly as romantic as you'd think.

"Oh, hey," Min said. "Where'd you go?"

Min is small and Asian, but she has a big presence. Being with her is like eating in a restaurant with some-one like Zooey Deschanel—you're always aware she's there and what she's doing. And she didn't sound like my mom just then, but that's the way it felt, given what I'd been doing with Boston.

"Nowhere," I said. Then, realizing I needed some kind of lie, I added, "I met a friend. Over on Capitol Hill."

I don't know why I wasn't honest with Min and Gunnar about hooking up with guys. Min is bisexual and so far to the left that we once got into an argument over whether it's even *possible* for a homeless person to be an asshole. Gunnar's straight, but he's the second least judgmental person I know (after Min). And I'd told them both that I'd hooked up with guys before. But only *in theory*—something I'd done in the distant, abstract past. They didn't know I'd done it *lately*, three or four times anyway. And it felt especially weird now, coming home right afterwards, having them wonder who I was with and what I'd done.

"What friend?" Min said, looking up.

"Huh?" I said.

"That you met?"

"Oh. This guy from work." Could I have possibly told a less convincing lie? Now I was desperate to change the subject. "What're you guys up to?"

The truth is, I was embarrassed. I don't think hook-ups are wrong exactly, but they don't feel quite right either. It's like opening a bag of Chips Ahoy! and only having a couple, and feeling good about your incredible willpower, but then spending the rest of the day passing through the kitchen and helping yourself to another cookie each time. I'd never thought of myself as the kind of guy who would do hook-ups. But you do it once, and you realize how easy it is, and it becomes kind of addictive. And before you know it, you've eaten the whole bag.

So I guess I did feel guilty. In high school, I'd helped start my school's first GSA, and it had been a really big deal. After that, I'd watched all the gay-themed episodes of *Glee*, usually with tears streaming down my face (I'd been fully aware at the time what a clunky, horribly-written show it was, but it didn't really matter, because the subject matter was obviously so revolutionary for television). Meanwhile, the rest of the LGBT community was working their butts off for marriage equality—coming out to friends and family, protesting, writing articles and making videos, talking to voters and politicians. Actors like Neil Patrick Harris and Zachary Quinto and Jesse Tyler Ferguson—and Ellen, don't forget Ellen—were risking their whole careers to come out, not knowing how people would react.

And then the weirdest thing in the world happened. People just...changed their minds about gay people. It was almost overnight. And by now, in 2014, everyone who wasn't a crazy Christian nutbag totally agreed with us (and was also now acting like they'd *always* agreed with us, like we LGBT folks were sort of stupid for acting like it was a big deal in the first place, which was actually rather annoying). The point is, we achieved one of the biggest, fastest, most sweeping social changes in, like, the history of the world.

And for what? All so I could take a fumbling, frenzied roll on a dusty Ikea futon with some guy I'd never even met before? There had to be more to it all than that. Didn't there? So what the hell was the answer?

"Particle astrophysics," Min said. She was answering my question from before about what she was doing. "Which sounds a thousand times more interesting than it is."

Min is smart—really smart. She finished her undergrad in two and a half years (with credits from high school) and was now well on her way to her PhD (in physics).

Gunnar looked up from his tablet. "Did you know that every single time they do a deep sea dive into the area below the photic zone, they discover dozens of new species? *Dozens*. Every single time!"

If Min is this huge presence in any room, Gunnar is the kind of guy who tends to blend in. He reminds me of actors who plays the postman in TV commercials. He's the sort of person who gets better-looking the longer you know him.

"And you know how some deep-sea animals grow to gigantic sizes?" Gunnar said. "Giant crabs, giant squid, giant stingrays? No one knows why. Isn't that fantastic? Science still hasn't explained it!"

In other words, Gunnar seems perfectly average, but only until he opens his mouth. He has this tendency to get obsessed about strange things. Once back in high school, he'd started growing mushrooms in the crawlspace of his house, but not hallucinogenic ones like a typical high school kid. No, Gunnar had been obsessed with the normal edible ones, like shiitakes and morels and chanterelles. Remember when I said that Gunnar didn't have to work? This was basically what he did all day instead of a job: just sort of geek out on things he found interesting. But he never stayed obsessed about any one thing for long. After he'd made all that money with his *Singing Dog* app, I'd practically had to beg him to do a follow-up app for Christmas, *Singing Dog: Jingle Bells* (alas, it tanked). Once he was done with one obsession, he simply moved on to the next one, which, lately, had been "deep-sea creatures"—those animals (and plants?) that live in the area of the ocean below where light reaches.

As long as I've been friends with Gunnar, people have said that he's off in his own little world, which is absolutely true, except I think this is a good thing while everyone else is totally judging him.

"Oh, hey, I forgot to tell you guys," Min said. "Guess what I heard?"

"What?" I said.

"The she-demons are moving."

This was what we called these two little old ladies who lived across the dock from us—they were sisters. Our falling out with them had started innocently enough. A year or so earlier, I'd made the mistake of shaking out a rug outside our houseboat, right after the two of them had just stained a deck chair. One of them had made a noise that, I swear, sounded like an animal dying.

I'd apologized—*profusely*. I'd even offered to buy them an entirely new deck chair. But it had all gone downhill from there anyway. Soon they were accusing us of stealing their hanging fuchsia, and complaining about the fact that our hose wasn't coiled right. Now every time we passed by their boat, we could feel them glaring at us—and sometimes you could even hear them softly muttering obscenities (no, seriously). The two of them were off in their own little world too, but unlike Gunnar, it was the Land of Crazy-Ass Old Ladies.

"They're really moving?" I said to Min, excited. "Really?"

"They're really moving," she said.

"Oh, my God, let's get turnt up!" I said. Basically, I was saying, "Let's party!" I was probably using the expression wrong. Then again, I'm the least hip twenty-three-year-old of all time.

"You know if they're selling or moving?" Gunnar asked Min. Unlike a house, you can literally *move* a houseboat, by unhooking it from the dock and pushing it out into the water.

"Neither," Min said. "They're going to just open a portal to hell and push their house directly over onto a lake of fire."

She said this so deadpan that it took a second for Gunnar and me to realize that she was joking. But then we got it. We all laughed.

"I bet I know why they're leaving," I said. "Whole Foods stopped carrying eye of newt."

Gunnar snorted. "Yeah, and their broomsticks kept colliding with the seaplanes landing out on the lake."

I laughed again. "They couldn't figure out how to make a houseboat out of gingerbread!"

"They realized they'd already eaten all the neighborhood kids!" Gunnar said.

These may not have been the most brilliant jokes ever, but we were all in the mood to laugh, so we did, a little bit like we were high. And the fact that Min was laughing right along with Gunnar's and my politically incorrect "witch" jokes shows how truly annoying these two women really were.

"I bet they'll find mummified bodies down in the basement," Min said.

"Absolutely not," I said, mock-soberly. Then I

waited a second or two and said, "Because houseboats don't have basements!"

"I think they cut up the bodies and dump them in the middle of Lake Union wrapped in plastic bags," Gunnar said, "like in *Dexter*."

I was laughing so hard now that my face hurt. I couldn't remember the last time I'd felt so good. It was even better than sex with Boston.

But then our laughter sort of tapered off. The boat rocked gently, and Min said, "Well, I hate to break up the party, but I should get to bed."

Gunnar folded up his tablet case. "Yeah, me too."

"Really?" I said, disappointed. I'd just got home, and I didn't want to go to bed yet. It had something to do with that hook-up with Boston—it had left me feeling strange. Lonely. Or maybe it was the fact that I liked Gunnar and Min so much. As tight as it could sometimes feel on that houseboat, I almost never got sick of them.

"Don't you have to work tomorrow?" Min said.

She was right—I did.

"Great," I said, grimacing. "Now you've torn the paper lantern off the light bulb." This was a Blanche DuBois reference, from that old play *A Streetcar Named Desire*, about how she's always trying to avoid the harsh light of reality by putting colorful paper lanterns over the bare light bulbs. And if there was any doubt before when I said that I'm the least hip twenty-three-year-old of all time, well, there clearly isn't now. (But hey, sometimes I do hook-ups!)

Gunnar and Min just groaned and rolled their eyes. I'd explained the Blanche DuBois reference before, and I said it now mostly to annoy them. But I put up with plenty of *their* quirks, so they could put up with a few of mine.

"Good *night*, Russel," Min said.

"Good night, Min," I said, smiling, as she and Gunnar trotted off to bed.

But I didn't go to bed. I hadn't taken a shower at Boston's, so I took one now (I had no choice: there's no bathtub in Gunnar's houseboat).

And I stood there under the hot water thinking about my life. I don't want to make this sound all maudlin or overly-dramatic. I mean, it's not like I was in tears or anything. Maybe I didn't have specific thoughts at all. It was more just a feeling. But if I had to put it into words, it was the feeling that my life hadn't turned out the way I'd expected.

I'd survived high school (no small accomplishment), and I'd gone to the University of Washington (and graduated magna cum laude with a double major in psychology and political science—also no small accomplishment, but small potatoes compared to surviving high school). But now what? What came next? When it came to my love life, it was pretty much non-existent—except for the five or six online hook-ups I'd done. Which isn't to say that hooking up with guys via iPhone apps had anything to do with "love" anyway.

Speaking of my friends, here was Gunnar owning a houseboat and not having to work, at least for the foreseeable future, just ticking off his fleeting passions, doing whatever the hell he wanted every day. And then there was Min, effortlessly plowing her way through her PhD like an ice-breaker through Arctic seas.

Between Min's unstoppable career drive and Gunnar's passionate aimlessness, they had their lives all figured out. But I still didn't have a clue about mine. I knew I was only twenty-three years old, but still.

So anyway, I'm standing there in that shower, haphazardly soaping myself up, feeling the hot water run off of me. And my nose started to bleed. I've always gotten a lot of nosebleeds—when I was a kid, the doctor had tried cauterizing my nose three times, where they try to burn the blood vessels in your nose (once with heat, twice with chemical cold), but it had never really taken. Now I always carry Kleenex with me wherever I go and sort of accept that my nose will start bleeding every few weeks. I'd call it my period, except I'm sure that's ridiculously sexist.

Anyway, I know how to stop a nose-bleed. You pinch your nose and wait for the blood to congeal (don't tip your head back! The blood will run down your throat). It's harder to do in the shower, with the hot steam and water all around you opening up blood vessels, but it always stops eventually.

But this time I didn't pinch my nose. I just let the blood drip down from my nose into the water swirling around the drain—drip, drip, drip. The blood didn't look red in all that water—it was more rust-colored. As soon as one drop would hit the white fiberglass floor, it would quickly wash away, but then another drop would follow right behind. I could taste the blood in my mouth, salty and coppery.

Drip, drip, drip—the blood kept dripping, but I still didn't stop it, didn't pinch my nose. After a while, it seemed to drip even faster. How much blood had fallen out of me already? It seemed like a lot. An eighth of a cup? A quarter cup? What would happen if I just let it keep dripping? Would it drip away forever? Would I bleed to death? Had anyone ever bled to death from a bloody nose? In the history of the world, had anyone ever committed suicide by not pinching off a nose-bleed in the shower?

Again, I don't want to get carried away here or go all goth on your ass. I wasn't really trying to kill myself. My life wasn't even that bad. Privileged white guy, remember? First World problems? And I'd literally just been having a great time with Min and Gunnar out in the front room, laughing so hard about the crazy old ladies next door that I'd almost pissed myself. And hey, I lived in a houseboat on Lake Union.

So before too long, I did finally plug my nose, and then I waited for the blood to congeal. It didn't take long for the nose-bleed to stop.

But the question that had been on my mind since coming home from Boston's apartment, that didn't go away: *What's the point of it all?*

And standing in that tiny on-board shower, in between those cheap fiberglass walls, I realized I didn't have the slightest clue.

CHAPTER TWO

I work two different jobs, about fifty hours a week total. What with student loans and paying rent to Gunnar (thanks, Min!), I don't have a choice. It sucks. It's a little like being the child of divorced parents. I have both jobs pulling at me, asking me to do something and implying that the whole world is going to end if I can't manage to make it work, even if what one is saying totally contradicts what the other is saying. I'm constantly having to choose, and no one is ever really satisfied, least of all me.

My first job is working as a lifeguard at Green Lake, which is this urban lake a couple of miles north of downtown. The whole lake is a surrounded by a park, and the city bans motorized boats on the water, so it's actually this weirdly peaceful little oasis in the middle of the busy metropolis. Most of the year, I work inside, in the indoor pool, but a couple of days before, in early June, the city had officially begun posting lifeguards at the two outdoor swimming areas, one at each end of the lake. And because the lake is this weirdly peaceful little oasis in the middle of the busy metropolis, hordes of people descend on it, especially on a sunny day.

The day after I got the bloody nose in the shower, I was working the swimming area on the west side of the lake. The lifeguard office is inside an old brick bathhouse (which sounds more impressive than it is). It looks out on a grassy sun-bathing area and these broad concrete steps that lead down to the lake itself. There are usually five lifeguards in total on duty, and we rotate every fifteen minutes, spending fifteen minutes at each of the three stations out on the lake and thirty minutes inside the office in the bathhouse, answering swimmers' questions and bullshitting with the other off-duty lifeguard.

It was a sunny day, but it was early in the summer, so the lake was crowded, but not insane. Even so, lifeguarding takes a lot more energy than most people think. You *really* have to pay attention, because if you phone it in, that's sure to be the day some snot-nosed brat hits his head on the dock and drowns.

I had just started one of my thirty-minute stints in the office. The other lifeguard was this guy named Clint—basically a stack of muscles wrapped in a sheath of bronze skin, topped with a tousled mop of brown, sun-highlighted hair.

"Oh, my Gawd!" he said. "I think I just nutted my chinos!"

He was talking about some hot girl out on the lake. How did I know this? Because hot girls out on the lake was all Clint *ever* talked about.

Sure enough, he was standing at the office's open half-door, looking out at the swimmers. "Do you see her? The girl in the yellow tankini?" He gripped his heart. "Oh, man!"

"Ha," I said, surprised that a guy like Clint even knew what a "tankini" was.

Then Clint glanced over at me and remembered for the hundredth time that I was gay. So he looked back out at the swimming area and said, "And what about the twin frat boys? You see *them*?"

I smiled. "Yeah." The truth is, unlike the girl in the yellow tankini, I knew exactly who Clint was talking about. They weren't really twins, but they were close enough.

For the record, if you've ever wondered if, behind our dark glasses, the lifeguards at a beach or lake are checking out all the people we're supposedly life-guarding, we totally are. Staring without consequence at hot young bodies in wet, clinging swimsuits is the one real perk of being a lifeguard.

"Seriously," Clint said. "I'd take a piece of *them*."

Clint always did this, every day we happened to be in the office together. He wouldn't just suddenly remember I was gay and then ask if I thought a particular guy was hot. No, he'd tell me, for my benefit, exactly which guys *he* thought were hot. Not that he'd ever act on it. Clint is what I think of as a Seattle Straight Boy. That means a guy who's fit, liberal, well-groomed—maybe a bit hipster/scruffy. Taken all together, you might assume a Seattle Straight Boy is gay. But he's not. Talk to him for more than two minutes, and it's immediately clear that he's completely, astoundingly straight. My theory is that at some point in the mid-00s, years before the rest of the world suddenly shifted on LGBT issues, word went out from Seattle women to all the straight guys that they were never getting laid again if they were even vaguely homophobic. So they changed. Like, overnight. Now they're almost *too* pro-gay. In fact, a lot of them like nothing better than flirting with gay guys, which is sort of what Clint was doing with me.

"So," I said. "Got any fun plans?" Talking hot guys with Clint made me uncomfortable, so I always changed the subject.

"Gonna do some kayaking on Lake Sammamish. Gotta head over to R.E.I. after work to pick up some stuff."

R.E.I. is short for Recreational Equipment Incorporated—*the* place to shop in Seattle for anything outdoor-related. It's also ground zero for Seattle Straight Boys.

That's when I remembered: Clint was a kayaker. And a biker. And a slackliner. And a surfer. And a rock-climber. Basically, if it took place outside and you could look butch doing it, Clint was right there.

"What about you?" Clint asked me.

"Me?" I said. Stalling for time, I reached for the sunblock. I have red hair—actually, more auburn—and fair skin. So of course I took a job as a lifeguard. I don't tan, but if I constantly slather on the sunblock, I never actually burn either. And—fringe benefit—all the sun clears up my zits.

"What you got goin' on?" Clint said. "Like, this summer."

We already covered this, right? The night before, when I was standing in that shower watching my life-blood drip away by the pint? I didn't have anything going on in my life, which was almost too pathetic for words.

So I said, "Nothing big." And I desperately wanted to change the subject again. But this time I couldn't think of anything to say. So I kept slopping on more sunblock like it was the most important thing in the world.

Before too long, we rotated lifeguard stations. Clint left, and I found myself in the office with Willa—a small, dark-skinned woman with tightly-bound hair. She and I had always been friendly enough. But unlike Clint, who was like a human pinball machine, she was snootier, more uptight.

Right then, she was tapping away on her laptop.

Click, click, click, click, click.

"What you working on?" I asked.

"Huh?" she said, not looking up. "Oh, nothing. My startup."

"Startup, huh?" I smiled. "Big plans?"

She looked up and sort of glared at me. "We already have a million dollars in angel investing."

"Wow. Congratulations." But now I was confused. "If you have all that money, why are you still working here?"

She was already back to typing—*click, click, click, click, click.* "I'm maxed out, and the first check doesn't come till September."

"Ah." Then I said, "A few summers ago, my best friend made nine hundred thousand dollars on an iPhone app."

Willa looked up at me again, like I'd finally said something interesting. "What about you?"

"What about me?"

"Do you design iPhone apps? Like your friend?"

"Oh. No." And then I started slathering on the sunblock again, not because I needed it now, but because I didn't want to answer any more questions. I was incredibly thorough, trying to look so busy that Willa wouldn't possibly interrupt me. And sure enough—*click, click, click*—she didn't.

But that's when it hit me. Min and Gunnar weren't the only two people my age who had a point to their lives. It seemed like everyone I knew did. Sure, it wasn't always big "career" ambition, like Min, working on her PhD at all hours of the night, or Willa, typing away on her startup even during brief office breaks. Sometimes it was like Clint, totally committed to his never-ending kayaking and slacklining adventures, or Gunnar, losing himself in his edible mushrooms or deep-sea creatures.

But those were basically the two choices: either Unstoppable Career Drive or Passionate Aimlessness.

Which made total sense when you thought about it. My generation had inherited all these massive, impossible problems: collapsing ecosystems, dysfunctional government, out-of-control corporations, crazed terrorists, slightly less crazed Tea Partiers, insane college tuitions, and the even more insane requirement that you get a college degree or you're totally screwed. So we were all looking at this big fucking mess of the world, and we were responding in one of two ways: eat, drink, and be merry (as much as possible given that climate change and/or Republican assholery was quickly going to destroy us all), or feverishly outwork and outsmart the competition in a desperate *Mad Max*-like battle royale over the last piece of the ever-dwindling pie.

How had I never seen all this before? It suddenly made so much sense that everyone around me was doing exactly what they were doing. What other choice did they have?

Okay, fine, the world sucked, and the way people my age were acting made sense. So now I knew why they were choosing either Unstoppable Career Drive or Passionate Aimlessness. But I still didn't know how they managed to pick between the two. And then, once they'd decided, how did they go about picking a specific career or a particular passion? Did the answer come to them one day from out of a burning bush? Or did they just randomly *pick* something, thinking, "Well, anything is better than nothing"?

I didn't know. Even worse, I had no idea how to go about finding it out. It was like there was some secret to life that everyone else knew, but that no one had ever bothered to tell me.

Was there? Part of me was tempted to ask Willa then and there, because it seemed like if anyone would know it, she would. On the other hand, then she'd also know I was even more pathetic than she already thought.

No, asking Willa was out. But one way or another, I was determined to figure this thing out.

It's always been hard for me to take my second job seriously. It's at a place called Bake, located in the U Village, which is this trendy shopping mall just north of the University of Washington. It's one of those stupid "gimmick" stores. In this case, it's sort of a bakery, but the idea is you create your own specialized loaf of bread. The store is full of these ceramic bins of things you can put in your bread: ordinary stuff like nuts, raisins, seeds, and dried fruit; quirky, supposed-to-be-good-for-you stuff like wheat germ, quinoa, flaxseeds, oats, and buckwheat; and decadent or truly weird-for-bread stuff like M&Ms, crushed potato chips, gummy worms, and tiny pretzels (oddly popular).

So these are your loaf's "integrants," which is a fancy, high-end word for "ingredients," and which totally confuses everyone, because they assume you're saying "ingredients" when you're not. The idea is for customers to pick their own "integrants," measuring them out in the recommended amounts with these little tin cups and putting them into their own plastic bin. Then they hand their bin to the guy working behind the counter—usually me—and I blend it up in one of six different pre-made, pre-risen bread doughs and pop it into these super-hot ovens, and ten minutes later, you have a loaf of bread that "you" "made" "yourself."

The whole thing is *just so stupid*. I mean, eight dollars (minimum) for a loaf of bread that you pretend you made? What sort of person *does* that?

Okay, okay, I realize there's nothing more boring than listening to someone bitch about his job. The only thing you really need to know about Bake is that my bosses are a married couple, Jake and Amanda, who also happen to own the store.

And they hate each other with the passion of a thousand suns.

That particular day, they were sniping at each other because of something that had happened before work—something to do with earbuds, like for an iPhone.

"I just don't know why you didn't pick it up," Amanda said. "You said you would."

"Because I forgot to put it on the list, okay?" Jake said. "What difference does it make? I'll do it tomorrow."

"The difference is, you broke yours, and you keep taking mine, and then I can't find it. That's what difference it makes."

"Well, why don't you pick one up then?"

"Why should I? You're the one who broke it."

"Okay, *fine*, I'll do it tonight."

"The Apple store will be closed by the time we close."

"Then what exactly would you like me to do?"

Was it buying and operating Bake that had condemned Jake and Amanda to their hell of a relationship? I didn't know, and I didn't really care. I just desperately wanted out of our daily reenactment of the Sartre play *No Exit*.

"Besides," Jake was saying to Amanda, "why do you keep saying that it was *my* earbud that broke?"

"Because it was! It was the one *you* were using."

"Oh, please. We've been using them interchangeably for months now."

"Yes, but it broke when *you* were using it! Is this really that difficult to understand? And, oh God, you didn't take the trash out like I asked you either."

"It's not even—"

"I'll do it!" I said suddenly.

Jake and Amanda both looked over at me.

"The trash," I said. "I'll take it out to the dumpster."

Then, before either of them could object, I grabbed the trash and left.

As sad as it sounds, on the days that I had a stint at Bake with Jake and Amanda together, I lived for the chance to take the trash out to the dumpster.

U Village is an outdoor mall, and the closest dumpster is a couple of hundred feet from the store, across a parking lot and behind an alley. There's no way Jake and Amanda could prove that I didn't get waylaid by a truck or a car, so I took my sweet time.

It was after dusk, but not quite night, and the air was cool and wonderful—the complete opposite of the stuffiness of the store. I caught a whiff of the ginger coming from the Chinese dumpling place, and it was wonderful to smell something other than baking bread.

The parking lot was surprisingly empty, which meant the mall was mostly deserted too.

Walking back to the store, my long-range sensors detected a hot guy at the far end of the mall corridor. He was so far away I didn't need to do my discreet double-take. I could stare openly, and he'd never know I was staring at him. From what I saw, he was really hot—dark, fit, sexy beard—but I couldn't really see his face, since he was still so far away.

I had to walk toward him to get back to Bake, so I did. He got clearer and clearer in my vision—and better and better looking. Even now, I was so far away that he couldn't possibly know that I was leering.

Then something clicked in my brain, and I realized this wasn't just some random hottie. I actually knew this guy. I'd *had sex* with this guy. (This was about the weirdest thing imaginable, seeing a hot guy, wondering what he looked like naked, and then realizing that you already knew.)

But it wasn't just that I'd seen him naked. I'd loved him. I'd never loved anyone like I did him.

The ground started rocking, but not like at home, because home was on a houseboat. Somehow the whole world was rolling.

It was Kevin Land, the first guy I'd ever been with, back in high school. I'd been sixteen years old when it had started, and yeah, we'd gone through a lot of teenage drama before we ended up together. But then we *had* been together, and it had been the most wonderful thing ever. People say a lot of things about young love—that it's strong, that it's pure, that it's innocent, and yeah, that it's stupid.

But here's the thing: it *is* those things, including the parts about it being strong and pure. Or at least it sometimes can be.

Love hadn't been like that since then, at least not for me. I'd dated a few guys in college, but there wasn't anyone who was particularly memorable and/or not completely crazy. And, well, you already know about the seven or eight times I've done online hook-ups. That was pretty much my love life over the last few years—about as satisfying as the rest of my life.

Kevin and I had gotten together for good in the spring of my junior year. And then we'd dated all through the rest of high school, and the summer following it too.

And it had been truly wonderful. It's not just that he was hot, or that we had good sex, although he was, and we did. And it's not just that he was a great guy, although he was that too: decent, honest, sensitive, non-crazy. It's how he made me feel, how I acted around him.

I'd been around plenty of awful couples in my life, some gay and some straight. Even when it wasn't a constant war like it was with Jake and Amanda, it just wasn't very nice to be around. Why did love turn people into such jerks?

But once in my life, it hadn't been like that. With Kevin. Or maybe it had been, but in reverse. He did or said something nice or thoughtful for me, which inspired me to do something nice or thoughtful for him. It was the opposite of a vicious cycle.

I don't want to exaggerate things. I mean, we had problems. We could both be pissy and insecure (especially me). We took each other for granted. Once I'd borrowed his iPod Mini, cracked the plastic, but then pretended it had been fine when I returned it.

But most of the time, he made me a better person.

Then we'd gone away to college. He'd gotten a baseball scholarship out of state. It was a great opportunity, and I wasn't about to let him pass it up, but I couldn't afford to follow him. I moved to Seattle and went to the University of Washington with Min and Gunnar. Even so, I knew that Kevin's and my love would last. It was just that strong, that pure, that innocent, and yeah, that stupid.

We Skyped and chatted and texted, and we saw each other on breaks and vacations. But I still lived near our hometown, so it was always *him* coming home to see *me*. And when, after a year or so, he didn't come home for every little vacation, I started to feel resentful.

We still Skyped and chatted and texted.

But I guess we started to change. He had his friends, most of whom I'd never even met. I had my friends. For a while, I didn't mind all the backstory that was required to make what he was telling me make sense. Then more and more it started to feel like a hassle.

Basically, my pissy, insecure side started to win out over my nice, thoughtful one. And as great as Kevin was, he changed too (probably because I was so pissy and insecure). Suddenly I was one half of one of those couples that I'd always hated spending time around. Only I couldn't volunteer to take the trash out to leave it behind, because I was one half of the problem.

Then one long weekend he'd said he couldn't come home. I don't even remember the reason, but I'm sure it was a good one. I mean, he'd come home as much as he could.

So basically, I said, "Fine, don't come home." I'm sure I was hoping he would say, "No, wait! I was wrong! Of course I'll come home!"

But he didn't. And not only did he not come home, he didn't Skype or chat or text me either. He probably thought I'd been a jerk about the whole thing (which I sorta had been), so he was expecting *me* to contact *him*.

I don't know why I didn't, not at first. I was still hurt, I guess. He'd been the one to not come home, so I expected him to sort of make up for it by being the first to start up the interaction again. But after I while, I mostly forgot about him not coming home for the weekend, and I was just annoyed that he wasn't contacting me. Over a dumb little thing like my wanting him to come home for the weekend?

Then again, I wasn't contacting him either. And somehow this stupid little misunderstanding grew into this massive point of pride. Before long, I was really, really pissed at him—absolutely furious. Looking back on it now, it all sounds so stupid. All I can say is that it made sense at the time.

Anyway, days turned into weeks, and neither of us contacted the other—not even a single "like" on Facebook. And months later, when I finally stopped being angry and I realized what a huge mistake I'd made, I guess I had too much pride to make things right. It was easier just to pretend the whole thing had never happened. Besides, I was certain he'd moved on. (I did mention what a total hottie he is, right?)

That was that. I never talked to him again.

And now here he was, right in front of me.

It's not like I stood there going over all this in my mind when I saw him. This is just important exposition you need to know.

No, I saw him, and I did hesitate for a second. But I'm no fool. I immediately started forward, desperate to talk to him, to apologize and beg his forgiveness.

But now, wouldn't you know it, there was a small crowd at the end of the mall, and he'd somehow disappeared inside it.

And of course, by the time I'd made it to the end of that outdoor mall, he'd disappeared completely.

CHAPTER THREE

So this just figured, right? I'm feeling all mopey and pointless-y about my life, and then I spot my ex from high school, who reminded me of the last time I didn't feel quite so pointless. But then when I try to talk to him, I can't find him.

If this was a movie, I'd now spend the rest of the story trying to track him down. But it's not a movie, which means smartphones and social media exist—always, not only when the plot needs them to. Hell, I still had Kevin's cellphone number in my phone. Maybe he'd changed it, but I doubted it. And I also had his email address, and his Skype name. Assuming he lived in Seattle now, I could even look up his actual address and just show up at his door.

The point is, I had a million ways to contact him. I could have called him right then and said, "Hey, this is Russel. I just saw you in U Village, and I wanted to say hi. I'm standing by the fountain made up of spitting frogs, where are you?"

But of course I didn't. Accidentally bumping into each other at the mall was one thing. Calling him or texting him or dropping him an email seemed like something else entirely.

I figured I could at least cyberstalk him, so I stood there in that shopping mall searching for him on Facebook on my phone. Then I remembered that at some point in the last few years, we'd unfriended each other. I don't remember who had done it first (okay, yes, I do: he did). But his impulse had been right: it was impossible for both of us to move on with our lives when we were constantly being confronted with pictures of each other looking adorable and inner-tubing up at Mount Shasta with his new boyfriend. That's probably why he'd set all his settings on "private" too.

I Googled him and found a couple of recent pictures of him. I wasn't sure whether he played baseball anymore, but now he ran marathons. That was cool.

Why wasn't I calling him? I needed to get back to Bake, for one thing. But mostly it was pride. Yes, I'd been a jerk, but he sort of had been too. So now I was supposed to go crawling back? All of a sudden that stupid old misunderstanding made sense again. It'd be one thing if I were successful now—if I'd invented a bestselling app, or were getting my PhD, or even if I ran marathons. But I worked two pathetic jobs I hated, had done nine or ten loveless online hook-ups, and occasionally stood in the shower trying to kill myself via nose-bleed.

Okay, yes, maybe I was feeling sorry for myself. But this was my fucking party, and I'd cry if I fucking wanted to.

*   *   *

When I got home from work late that night, Min was in the front room studying with her grad school friends Trai and Lena. Trai is this small Asian guy in hipster horn-rims and skinny jeans. Lena is small and skinny too, with long, straight brown hair—sort of an anemic flower child with blocky, tortoiseshell glasses.

Truthfully, it's always a little disorienting to spend the day around all those fit, tan bodies at the lake, and then come home to Min and her skinny, pasty grad school friends. It's also weird how the three of them all sort of blend together, with their flat hair and dark earth tones. Sometimes I thought of Trai and Lena as Min's "Min-ions," mostly because of how much the two of them resembled her.

"Hey, guys," I said, squeezing my way into the kitchen. From there, I could see that the three of them were analyzing scatter plot charts on their iPads. Living on a houseboat is great and everything, but the problem comes whenever you invite more than one person over. Then it's suddenly like spending three hours in a crowded elevator.

"What's for dinner?" Min asked me.

I held up the take-out I'd picked up at Than Brothers on the way home—this local chain of Vietnamese restaurants. I'd ordered an extra large chicken pho with extra vegetables.

"I always order exactly the same thing," I said. "But they always charge me something different. It's never more than fifty cents either way, but still."

"Vietnamese charge by the mood," Trai said, and I was a little afraid to smile. I guess he could say that, because he's Vietnamese.

"Anyone want some?" I said, mostly just being polite.

"No, thanks," Min said.

Trai snickered, and I realized that Lena had just sent him a text message through her iPad. Had it been about me?

Here's where I should probably point out that I didn't like Trai and Lena very much. The weird thing was, I couldn't really pinpoint why. I just always had a sense that they didn't like me first. Maybe it was all in my mind. I mean, why did I assume Lena's text message was about me?

"So how was your day?" Min asked. She hadn't looked up from her iPad, but she sounded sincere.

Truthfully, I wanted to take my pho into my sleeping loft and eat it alone on the futon. But it was going to take a few minutes to reheat in the microwave.

"I ran into Kevin Land," I said. "Out at U Village."

Min's face jerked up. "*Seriously?* How'd *that* go?" She knew my whole history with him.

"I didn't talk to him. I just saw him from afar."

"Is he living in Seattle now?" Min turned to Lena and Trai. "Kevin was this guy that Russel used to go out with in high school." Trai is straight (but not really a Seattle Straight Boy), and I was pretty sure Lena was bisexual like Min.

They didn't nod or look up or anything, just kept working.

"Who knows?" I said to Min. "I unfriended him a long time ago."

"What are you going to do? Are you going to talk to him?"

"I don't know." I really didn't. I decided to take the high road and try and include Trai and Lena in the conversation. "You guys are the physicists. Isn't there a theory that everything that could happen has already happened?"

Lena and Trai exchanged a glance. Trai typed something, and now I saw a text message pop up on Lena's iPad.

"Well, sort of," Min said.

"In that case, I already met Kevin," I said. "And I'm sure it was a complete disaster."

Min smiled.

"But maybe I should," I said. "Maybe the universe is drawing the two of us back together again."

"Maybe it is," Min said.

"What's that theory?" I said. "That we're all connected?"

"We're all connected in lots of ways," Trai said. "The atoms in our body have electromagnetic forces. There are forces in the universe that drive everything together, even as other forces push us apart."

Tell me about it, I thought.

"And there's the idea that there's really no such thing as 'solid' matter—that we're all just energy fields, exchanging atoms with everything around us. That the divisions we see are just a matter of perception. We're constantly exchanging atoms."

That made me wonder: Did I still have any of Kevin's atoms inside me? It had been years since we'd been together, but at the time, we'd exchanged a lot more than atoms, if you know what I mean. (After getting tested! And having lots of serious talks about what it "meant.")

"Isn't there a theory that explains the whole world?" I said. "Or at least *tries* to?"

"The Theory of Everything," Trai said.

"Well, does the Theory of Everything say whether or not I should call Kevin?"

"Sadly, no," Min said.

"It's not that kind of theory," Trai said. "It's a theoretical framework to understand physics—to explain all physical aspects of the universe."

No shit, Sherlock! I thought. *'Cause I totally thought it would tell me whether to call my ex-boyfriend.*

"Well, you guys need to keep searching then," I said. "Come up with a new theory that explains it, okay?"

"Yeah, we'll get right on that," Min said, smiling.

Part of me wanted to go on talking, to ask Min and her friends outright what I'd been thinking about before—how everyone seemed to know the secret to life except me. But I knew this wasn't the time.

The microwave dinged. My pho was done, which meant I could take my dinner and get the hell out of Dodge.

The front door opened. It was Gunnar, coming home from—where? He didn't have a job. And yet, he was almost always gone during the day. So where did he go? I'd never really asked him. Then again, I doubted he'd give me a straightforward answer if I did.

"Hey, there," I said to him. I nodded to my pho. "Hungry?"

"Nah," he said. He sort of shuffled his feet, and the boat rocked a little, almost like he'd caused it.

"Everything okay?" Min said to Gunnar.

He did look distracted. He almost always looks distracted—usually by something like a dead fly on the windowsill. But this was different. Now he seemed upset.

"Yeah," Gunnar said, hesitating.

Fortunately, the Min-ions weren't so annoying that they couldn't take the hint.

"We should go," Trai said.

"Yeah," Lena said.

It took them a minute to close out their programs and fold up their iPads, but then they were gone.

By now, Gunnar had taken a seat on the sofa in the main room. He was staring out the window. But it was dark out, so I doubted he could see anything.

There was an expression on Gunnar's face I'd never seen before. It was so stark, like a despairing Norwegian in some weary art house film. Outside, something sloshed.

Min and I exchanged a concerned glance. Gunnar had never acted like this before. It was like he was one of those guys who gets hit by a baseball, then suddenly speaks perfect French. On the other hand, we were his two best friends, and we totally wanted to be there for him, to do whatever we needed to do to help him.

This is it, I thought. This was the moment when Gunnar finally started acting like a normal person, when Gunnar grew up. What had happened? Had he learned he was adopted? That he was the product of rape? That he only had six weeks to live?

With her iPad put aside and my pho forgotten, Min and I took seats across from him.

"So," I said to Gunnar, softly. "What's up?"

He turned and stared at us—lost in his thoughts, adrift on some mysterious sea.

There was a pause, like the whole universe was holding its breath.

Then Gunnar said, "There are dozens of documented cases of American Indian tribes in the northwest warning early settlers of half-men/half-beast creatures that lived in the wilderness. 'Sasquatch' comes from the word 'sásq'ets' in the First Nations language of British Columbia."

There was another pause. Min and I didn't say anything. We exchanged another glance, but not so gentle and concerned this time. Now we were just confused.

Finally, I said to Gunnar, "What?"

"Bigfoot," he said. "I think it might be real."

Min's and my confusion was quickly giving way to annoyance.

"What does Bigfoot have to do with anything?" I asked.

Now Gunnar was the one confused. "What do you mean?"

"What does that have to *do* with anything?" Min said.

"Why does it have to do with something?" Gunnar asked. Now *he* had the nerve to sound annoyed with *us*.

"We thought you were upset about something," I said. "That you needed to talk."

"I *am* upset. Can you imagine what the existence of Bigfoot would mean? Why aren't more people studying it?"

That's when I finally really understood what was going on. Gunnar had found a new obsession. He'd shifted over from deep-sea creatures to the existence of Bigfoot.

Min and I both fell back in our seats at the same time, disgusted. (I should point out that Min seemed a lot *more* disgusted, but that was sort of typical. She didn't put up with a lot of shit.)

I realized how stupid I'd been to think that Gunnar was upset about something real. When would I finally accept that Gunnar wasn't normal—that he was never going to *be* normal?

"Bigfoot doesn't exist," Min said wearily.

Gunnar sat upright. "How can you *say* that? How can you definitively say it doesn't exist? I'm not saying it *does* exist—I'm just saying it *might*. That we should at least consider the evidence. That's what scientists are supposed to *do*, right? They keep an open mind. But most scientists won't even consider the evidence."

"That's just it," Min said. "There *is* no evidence. Only superstition, misidentification, and hoax."

"What about the stories from American Indian cultures?"

"Come on. Almost every culture has a myth about a half-man, half-beast creature. It's one of the 'cultural universals'."

"The what?" I said.

"Traits or beliefs that almost every culture on Earth shares," Min said. "Think about it. A belief in the 'wild man' concept could have been a way for earlier cultures to make sense of the idea that there was a connection between humans and the rest of the natural universe. Or maybe it was even our first vague understanding of evolution."

"Or!" Gunnar said. "Maybe it's evidence that creatures like that really existed! And maybe they still do."

"Gunnar," Min said.

"That's not the only evidence that Bigfoot exists," Gunnar said. "There's lots of other stuff."

"Like what?" I said. Let's face it: Gunnar's obsessions were weird, but they were usually pretty interesting. At the same time, I didn't have a dog in this hunt, and I still hadn't had dinner, so I stepped back toward the kitchen where my rapidly cooling pho was waiting.

"Gunnar," Min said. "Bigfoot doesn't exist."

"How do *you* know?"

"Well, because primates don't live outside the tropics, for one thing."

"Sure, they do."

"Are you talking about that species of monkey in Japan? That's not exactly the same thing."

"I'm talking about humans!" Gunnar said. "And not just contemporary humans—early humans too. And Neanderthals."

Min sighed. At first I didn't understand why she cared one way or the other what Gunnar thought of Bigfoot. Then I remembered how Gunnar had scared Min and me, how we'd thought that something was seriously wrong. Min was still annoyed. Plus—let's face it—she kind of likes to argue.

At this point, I'd like to point out that we didn't spend *all* our time on Gunnar's houseboat having stupid, irrelevant debates like this—over the Theory of Everything and Bigfoot.

I'd *like* to point that out, but I can't, because we pretty much *did* talk about stuff like this all the time. This was what happened when you put three twenty-something dorks together in the same ridiculously small houseboat. It was like some kind of reality TV show—the lowest rated reality TV show of all time, but still.

"It would be impossible for a creature the size of Bigfoot to have escaped discovery all these years," Min was saying.

"Scientists didn't discover the megamouth shark until 1991," Gunnar said, "and that grows up to eighteen feet long. The pygmy beaked whale wasn't discovered until 1987." Clearly, he'd been doing his research.

"Totally different," Min said. "Those are sea creatures."

"Okay, the mountain gorilla. Scientists didn't confirm its existence until the early twentieth century."

"Again, completely different. Bigfoot supposedly coexists in some of the most populated places on Earth."

"Yeah, which is why we have all these eyewitness accounts," Gunnar said. "Tell me how you account for *them*."

"A combination of misidentification and hoax. Even Bigfoot enthusiasts agree that *most* Bigfoot sightings aren't 'Bigfoot' at all, right? They're either fakes, or misidentification, or figments of people's imaginations. So why couldn't the remaining five percent of sightings be one of those things too?"

"They could! But we don't *know* they are. That's all I'm saying. And some of them are compelling. Have you read the accounts? Seen the photos? The film?"

"I hope you don't mean the Patterson-Gimlin film," Min said. "Come on. We've now heard from the guy who says he made the monkey suit, and the guy who says he was *inside* the suit. But people still believe that film is real. Which, if you ask me, is the biggest reason of all to think that Bigfoot doesn't exist. People want it too badly. And that means we can't trust anything most people have to say."

I confess, Min had impressed me. "How in the world do you know stuff like this off the top of your head?" I asked her, even as I slurped on rice noodles.

"Oh, please," Min said. "Scratch a skeptic, and two millimeters down you find an idealist. I want Bigfoot to be true just as much as you do, Gunnar."

"*No!*" he said suddenly. "You *don't* want that! You don't care if Bigfoot exists *at all!*"

Gunnar was like a cat when you rub him the wrong way—perfectly fine one second, then seriously put out the next. Once again, he'd caught both Min and me by surprise. But unlike a cat, he didn't calm down again, immediately distracted by something else. On the contrary, Gunnar looked downright pissed. He jerked up out of his chair and stormed from the room. When he reached his bedroom on the lower half of the boat, he even sort of slammed the door.

And I was left to stare, bug-eyed, at Min and think: Someday someone really might capture a live Bigfoot and learn all about this mysterious new species, but never in a million years would I ever understand Gunnar.

CHAPTER FOUR

That weekend, I was back at work lifeguarding at Green Lake.

"Did you see the redhead in the two-piece?" Clint said when we were sharing the office again. Then the light bulb went off over his head for the zillionth time, and he looked back outside. "And hey, what about the DILF with the hairy chest? Pretty hot."

Later, I was taking my stint in one of the lifeguard chairs overlooking the swimming area. The lake was surprisingly crowded for such an overcast day— maybe fifty people in the water at any given time. Behind me, up by the bathhouse, someone was playing ragtime on the Green Lake piano, which is this upright piano a theater company rolls into the park on summer days, with a sign that says: *Play me.* Meanwhile, there was this guy walking around the swimming area in a tiny g-string carrying another sign that read: *Free kisses!* He might've had some takers if he'd looked like Channing Tatum, but alas, he was kind of flabby. The truth is, he looked like a pervert getting off on exposing himself to the crowd. On the other hand, he was staying, just barely, on the right side of "acceptable behavior" in a swimming area, so we couldn't tell him to leave, even if he was freaking out all the parents. Would it have made a difference if he'd had a boner in that g-string? Probably. For the record, it is exactly these kind of complicated, King Solomon-like judgment calls that the city is paying its lifeguard professionals nine-forty an hour to make.

But that would be a call for the office lifeguard anyway. I was in the lifeguard chair, so I was trying hard to ignore all that, determined to stay in the "lifeguard zone," the mental state where a lifeguard somehow manages to keep track of a hundred different people all at the same time.

An Earth-mother-type played with her toddler at the edge of the lake.

A ten-year-old girl stood waist-deep in the water while eating an ice cream bar.

Four teenage boys played a loud game of King of the Floating Dock.

A woman in a pink bathing cap did the crawl stroke out beyond the dock.

The aforementioned DILF with the hairy chest struggled to put water-wings on his four-year-old son.

The lifeguard zone isn't a conscious thing exactly. Yes, you "see" all the people in the lake in front of you, but they don't really register (unless they're hot, like the DILF). It's more of a "big picture" thing. You somehow keep the mental image of everyone together in your head. Then if something goes wrong, you notice it—intuitively or whatever.

(That said, I *was* totally aware that the little girl in pigtails was currently peeing in the lake. People who think they can pee and no one will know? The lifeguard knows. You can tell by the person's expression. We lifeguards just don't say anything, because, well, what exactly are we going to say? But for the record: ewwwww.)

I scanned the swimming area, back and forth, over and over again, trying to stay in the lifeguard zone. But after a while, my mind began to wander.

The label said that this sunblock wouldn't run and sting my eyes, but it totally does.

Man, that carp made a big splash. I'd like to kick the idiot who first released non-native species into Green Lake.

I wonder if I'll ever run into Kevin again.

I kept staring out at the lake even as ragtime kept playing on that piano.

Something is wrong, I thought.

I didn't know exactly what it was, but it was something. That was the thing about the lifeguard zone, or maybe about the human brain in general. Even when you're not looking at each individual person, even when your mind is wandering, you still notice when something's not right. And right then, my Spidey-sense was tingling something fierce.

I scanned the lake again, concentrating, trying to figure out exactly what was different.

The Earth-mother was still playing with her toddler.

The ten-year-old girl had finished her ice cream bar (and left the wooden stick floating in the water).

The boys were still playing King of the Dock.

The DILF was watching his son.

Even the little girl in pigtails, finally done peeing, looked a-okay.

The woman in the pink swimming cap. Where is she?

I looked to where she'd been before, and to where

she'd be now if she'd kept on her former swimming trajectory.

There were bubbles in the water.

Down below the bubbles was a dark form, not moving. There were no logs or rocks that big anywhere in the swimming area—I knew that for sure. And the dark form was way too big to be a giant carp or a turtle.

It's the woman.

I stood up and blew my whistle as loud as I could. I didn't turn to the other lifeguards positioned around the swimming area, or the ones back in the office, but if they did their jobs right, they'd step forward, seeing if I needed help, but also making sure to watch *everyone else* in the swimming area. Believe it or not, it's times like these, when the entire swimming area is focused on one lifeguard helping someone who's gone under, that some other kid could slip or be pushed under the water, and no one would notice. Back in the office, the lifeguards should already have been calling 911. (We lifeguards all hate our job, but we also know how important it is, and we take it pretty seriously.)

I climbed down from the lifeguard chair, keeping my eyes locked on those bubbles out in the lake. I kicked off my flip-flops, and ran for the water.

The lake is shallow right offshore—perfect for little kids futzing around in a swimming area, but too shallow for a lifeguard like me to make a running dive.

So I kept running, the water splashing up from my ankles, until I could finally make the dive.

Then I swam, keeping my head up, face forward, my eyes locked on the spot where the bubbles had been—bubbles that were already disappearing. From this angle, with the sun on the water, I couldn't really see the dark form anymore. This is why it's so important to never look away from the spot where you think the person is, not even for a second.

I dove down into the lake. I kept my eyes open underwater, and even though the lake is murky, I could see the woman's pale white skin and the blue of her one-piece swim-suit (but not the pink of her bathing cap). She wasn't moving, just drifting under the water, which meant she was unconscious.

I knew she hadn't been diving off a dock or near the diving board, that she'd been swimming the crawl stroke only minutes before, so there was no real danger of a back injury. Right now the most important thing was to get her out of the water and breathing again, so I reached out and grabbed her in the lifesaving hold (one arm over her shoulder from behind, around her body, and then under the armpit). Once I had her tight, I furiously kicked my way up again.

She was heavier than I expected, difficult to drag. That could mean her lungs were already full of water—very bad news.

My head broke the surface.

Still gripping the woman with one arm, I stroked with my other arm, and furiously kicked my way toward shore.

Once I was in the shallow water, I dragged her up onto the small rocky beach where I could stretch her out and start doing mouth-to-mouth and CPR if necessary. She was older than I expected, in her sixties at least.

By now, two of the other lifeguards from the

office had joined me. We turned the woman onto her side, to see if we could drain the water out of her mouth. Then we rolled her back again, and I tilted her head back to open the airway.

As soon as I did that, she started coughing, then gasping for air. This is exactly what they'd said might happen when I'd learned mouth-to-mouth. If it *hadn't* happened, her situation would have immediately been a hell of a lot more serious.

Another lifeguard appeared with a red wool blanket, pulling her upright, wrapping it around her, comforting her, telling her that help was coming. That's when I realized that at some point whoever had been playing the Green Lake piano had stopped. Everything was eerily quiet—so much so I could hear people breathing.

That's also when I realized what had happened, everything I'd just done.

Talk about being in the lifeguard zone! I'd barely had a conscious thought the whole time I'd been saving her. I definitely didn't remember making any actual decisions. I'd just seen what needed to be done and did it. But now it was hitting me what a big deal my job was, and how easily I could have screwed it all up. The world started to spin. I even started shaking. Maybe it was some kind of adrenaline withdrawal.

But then sirens rose in the distance, focusing me once again.

Lifeguards don't actually save that many people from drowning. I'd never done it before—except in the reach-for-a-small-kid-having-trouble kind of way. It had only happened to anyone three other times in the entire two years I'd been a lifeguard at Green Lake. So it was kind of a big deal that I'd done it, and so flawlessly.

I guess you could say I was kind of a celebrity, at least for that day. Of course I wasn't so much of a celebrity that anyone offered to give me the rest of the day off, or the next day either. But the other lifeguards were totally cool, high-fiving me and generally carrying on like I was a rock star. And as I worked my shifts in the office and out in the lifeguarding rotation, almost about every single person who had been swimming in Green Lake that day came up to me to thank me or congratulate me for a job well done (including the DILF—yeow!—and the "free kisses" guy, though I politely declined the kiss. Isn't that life for you? It's always the guy in the creepy g-string offering the free kiss, not the hairy-chested DILF in the board shorts. Why is that?).

Toward the end of the day, when I was back up in one of the lifeguard chairs again, a woman with white hair, sort of a bowl cut, came up and stood next to me. I was totally expecting her to fawn and dote, like all the other women had so far.

But she just looked up at me and smiled.

"You!" I said.

It was the lady from the lake, the woman I'd saved. She was shorter than I am, but lean and fit, maybe a little wide in the rear. Her face was tan with freckles, and wrinkled, but not leathery. She was wearing clothes now—blue jeans and a purple pull-over. She actually looked great.

"Are you okay?" I said. "Did you go to the hospital?"

She kept smiling. "I did, and I'm just fine, thanks to you. I had something called a shallow water blackout—apparently quite common in, *ahem*, older folks. Anyway, everything was fine, so they called a taxi to take me home. But I wanted to come back here and thank you."

Ordinarily, when someone tries to talk to you when you're sitting in one of the lifeguard's chairs, you're supposed to tell them to go talk to the office. But I wasn't about to say that to her.

"You don't have to thank me," I said, embarrassed (but secretly proud).

"Of course I do," she said. "You saved my life."

"No," I said.

"How exactly do you figure?"

"Well, yeah, okay, I did, but it's just part of my job."

"That doesn't matter. You still saved my life. And I wanted to thank you by having you over for dinner."

"Dinner?"

"Tomorrow night? You can bring whoever you want—another lifeguard? Or a friend. Or two? Or maybe a girlfriend? Or a boyfriend?"

She was telling me I could bring a boyfriend to dinner at her place? Part of me was a little offended, thinking, *Why would she assume I was gay?* But even as I thought this, I knew that's not what it was. She was simply a cool Seattleite who didn't want to make any assumptions. You could tell that from her whole demeanor.

"I'd be happy to come to dinner," I said. "But I think it'll just be me."

* * *

Her name was Vernie Rose, and she lived on Queen Anne Hill, which is one of the older (and more expensive) parts of town.

I had absolutely no idea what to expect, but I wasn't nervous exactly. At one point, I wondered if maybe she was an older woman who got her kicks by seducing young guys, like Stifler's Mom in *American Pie*, or maybe Mrs. Robinson in that old movie *The Graduate*. Or maybe she'd be a crazy eccentric, like Kathy Griffin, or the two wacky aunts on *Sabrina the Teen-Aged Witch*, and she'd end up giving my life meaning by introducing me to fine wine and the art of rumba dancing.

Her house was small, a green Victorian with beige trim and a red door. But unlike most of the others on the block, its paint was chipped and faded. There was a widow's watch on the second floor, and for the first time I wondered if Vernie was married. I suspected she wasn't, but I wasn't sure why.

"Russell!" she said when she answered the door, excited, but not creepily so. "Come in, come in." She was wearing an oversized dark green shirt—a cross between a button-down and a smock—and she had her short hair pulled back. At least she wasn't in a push-up bra. And it's not like she was wearing a kimono or a turban.

The house itself had hardwood floors and dried flowers and lots of bookshelves. Something smelled good from the kitchen—fish with dill?—but it was also clear she had a cat.

I complimented her on her house, and she thanked me. Then she said, "So. What's your drink?"

"My what?"

"Your drink! Everyone has a drink. It's part of who you are, it defines you. One's drink is very important, because it helps tell other people who you are."

"I don't..."

"Oh, of course you do! What do you order when you go out to a bar with your friends?"

"Um, I don't really go out to bars."

Behind cat-eye glasses, she glared at me, hard.

"A beer?" I said.

She shook her head. "Nope. That's what you order because you're too poor to afford your real drink."

"What if I really like beer?"

"You don't."

I shrugged and sort of nodded. She happened to be right.

"You have a drink," she said, "you just don't know what it is yet."

Yet another thing everyone knows but me, I thought.

"Don't worry," Vernie said. "That's a lot better than the posers who try to pretend that their drink is something other than what it really is—the whole 'double bourbon' crowd. It's just so tiring."

I actually found this somewhat reassuring.

Vernie gave me the fish-eye, considering. Finally, she announced, "I think you just might be a whiskey sour."

"That sounds about right," I muttered.

"Ha! I knew it. Whiskey sour, it is."

She stepped to the bar—how had I not noticed she had a bar with two stools in her front room?—and started pouring. Finally, she handed me the glass.

I took a sip. It was strong, but sweet—and sour, which I guess made sense.

She looked at me expectantly.

"I like it," I said. "I like it a lot." I really did. But was it "my drink"? That seemed like a lot of pressure to put on a glass of alcohol.

"If you like it, it's your drink," Vernie said. "At least for the time being."

"The time being? But I thought you said that everyone had to have a drink—that it helps tell people who I am."

"It does. But it would be a pretty sad world if people never changed, don't you think?"

I couldn't deny it.

"But I should point out that I cheated," Vernie said. "A whiskey sour is usually made with an egg white, and I was too lazy to go into the kitchen to get one."

"Well, that's a *huge* disappointment," I said, totally selling it.

"I know," she said, playing along.

"I mean, now how do I know if this is really my drink? Or maybe my drink is a whiskey sour without the egg white. How could you have done this to me? I'm so confused!"

"My irresponsibility knows no bounds."

I mock-turned away. "I can hardly stand to look at you. I'm blinded by the harsh light of reality. You've ripped the paper lantern off the light bulb."

Vernie's face cracked wide open. "Oh, Blanche Dubois in *A Streetcar Named Desire*! I love that play. People who say that Vivien Leigh was wrong for the part in the movie completely miss the irony that she could very well be Scarlett O'Hara twenty years later."

I got that irony! I wanted to say. Did the fact that I'd finally met someone who understood my *A Streetcar*

Named Desire references mean that she *was* Blanche DuBois—that Vernie was a desperate woman determined to seduce me in order to deny her own fading youth? It didn't seem likely, but I still couldn't be sure.

Vernie returned to the bar and held up a drink of her own. Not surprisingly, it fizzed.

"I," she said dramatically, "am a champagne cocktail."

I laughed out loud. "Somehow that doesn't surprise me."

"I'm going to tell you something, Russel, but you have to promise not to think I'm crazy."

"Okay," I said.

"No, I mean it! You have to promise. You have to not think I'm a barking-mad old lady. You promise?"

"I promise," I said, making a sign that was somewhere between cross-my-heart and the Boy Scout oath.

She stared at me for a second, sipping her champagne cocktail. Then she said, "You saved my life, correct?"

I shrugged again. I had a feeling I was going to be doing a lot of shrugging tonight.

"Well, I dreamt last night that I was going to save your life too. After all, I owe you."

At that, she stared at me. I wasn't sure what I was supposed to say, but suddenly I had a sinking feeling, like I was being set up for an Amway pitch.

"No, no!" Vernie said, reading the discomfort on my face. "You just promised you'd hear me out, that you wouldn't think I was barking mad."

"You're right, I did. So how? How are you going to save my life?"

"I don't know yet. The dream wasn't clear. Only that I would."

I swirled the ice cubes in my glass. "Maybe you already have. I mean, you've already found me my drink."

Vernie smiled. "Don't go anywhere. I've got to go spend a penny."

"Spend a penny?" I said.

"'Pee.' It's British."

She headed off to the bathroom, and that's when I finally knew: Vernie was no Blanche DuBois, or even Stifler's Mom. But she was definitely in the running for Kathy Griffin.

Vernie had made salmon for dinner, along with asparagus and a pretty flavorful rice and pea dish. It was just impressive enough to seem like a heartfelt thank you, but not so extravagant that it felt desperate.

"So just so you know," I said as we ate. "I don't have a girlfriend or a boyfriend. But if I did, it would be a boyfriend."

Vernie looked at me, confused.

"Yesterday at the lake?" I said. "You said I could bring a girlfriend or a boyfriend to dinner tonight. Well, I'm gay."

"Oh, please, you really think you had to tell me that? After the comment about the paper lantern and the light bulb?"

I shrugged. See? I'd predicted I'd be doing a lot of shrugging that night.

"But I'm glad you told me," she said. "All the interesting men are gay."

"You clearly haven't met my buddy Gunnar."

She dismissed it with a wave of her fork. "The exception that proves the rule. Trust me, I've been around enough to know. When did you first realize?"

"That I was gay?"

She nodded, and I had to think about that. People had asked me that question before, but I had a feeling Vernie was looking for something different, a more real kind of answer.

"I remember when I was just a little kid," I said. "I mean, like, four or five years old, not too long after I learned to read and write my name. I saw that this guy had the same name as I did, but he spelled it with only one 'l'. 'Russel,' not 'Russell.'" Here I made a point to emphasize the second "l". "And I must have known—maybe my parents told me—that that was unusual, that most people spelled it with two 'l's. But I really liked it. I told my parents I wanted to spell it with one 'l' too. They just sort of laughed, thinking I'd forget about it. I mean, I was five. But I didn't forget. I made a huge deal about it. I really, really wanted to spell Russel with one 'l'. I think it was because on some level I knew I was different, and I wanted other people—my parents—to know it. I didn't know *how* I was different—I wouldn't have said I was gay if anyone had asked. But I just knew on some fundamental level that I wasn't like everyone else. Anyway, finally my parents said, okay, spell it how you want. I mean, what difference did it make? It's a perfectly acceptable spelling. It's not like they changed my birth certificate or anything.

"So I grew up, right? I got older and older. And all through grade school, every time someone spelled my name, a teacher or something, it was always with two 'l's. And I had to correct them—I had to say, no, I only spell it with one 'l'. And maybe it was all in my imagination, but it seemed to me that people would sort of roll their eyes and go, 'Oh, one of *those* people, huh? Gotta be different.' And by now I'm slowly figuring out why I feel so different from everyone else, that I'm gay, and also that I'm this bookish, overly-sensitive geek of a guy who loves Tennessee Williams plays, and this is all stuff I definitely *don't* want people to know, not in a million years. So I'm feeling more and more awkward every time someone asks me to spell my name—like I'm telling them this secret that I really don't want them to know, or at least giving them a big hint. At one point, this guy at school actually said, 'Here comes the fag who spells Russel with one "l"!' And of course I totally panicked. I even went to my parents and said I wanted to change it back—that's when I found out they had never officially changed it. In the end, I decided it was too much of a hassle to change it again. And besides, I quickly realized that changing it would be way too suspicious. When you *are* gay, at least if you're the kind of gay guy who can pass for straight, you become really, really good at knowing exactly what looks suspiciously gay.

"Anyway, I came out eventually—that's a whole other story I don't want to bore you with here. And now I'm really glad I didn't change it. I love that I spell my name with one 'l'. It's like this secret conversation between me and my five-year-old self. He's telling me, 'Hey, I have all these feelings I don't understand, what do they mean?' And by embracing it, by being so proud of that one 'I', I'm validating him, telling him, 'Kid, you are great absolutely the way you are, even if you and everyone else won't understand it for another ten years.'"

Vernie just stared at me for a long time, this little smile playing along her lips.

"What?" I said.

"Nothing. That story was just too perfect. What else is there to say? You just told me everything I need to know about you. Anything else you said would be anticlimactic, so let's just end the meal here." She started to stand. "You wanna clear the table? Then I'll walk you to your bus."

I laughed out loud again. This was something else I was doing a lot of this evening—laughing.

"Can we at least finish dinner?" I said, taking a bite. "It's fantastic, by the way."

"Thanks." She sat back down again. "So. Are you seeing anyone?"

I thought about telling her about Kevin, but I knew what she'd say, that I needed to *call* him—that I needed to cram life into the juicer and drink it down (or something along those lines). I wasn't ready to hear that, so I said, "No, not now."

We ate in silence for a bit. Then Vernie said, "It's funny how being gay is no big deal anymore, at least in cities like Seattle. Which is just great. I mean, I voted for Hope and Change. Go-bama! Equality forever! But what if being outsiders and misunderstood is part of what made gay men so interesting? God knows it's misery and suffering that made so much music so great—jazz and the blues. Joni

Mitchell had polio as a child—it weakened her hand, so she had to figure out how to retune the guitar and re-finger the cords. And *that's* what gave her that distinctive sound and all those unusual harmonies. But then I remember what it was like being a woman in Hollywood, and I think, 'Screw misery and suffering!' They'll always be pain in the world. Why not eliminate as much of it as we can? If gay boys and girls start to grow up as boring and conventional as everyone else, well, that means we *won*."

I nodded. I'd had all these exact same thoughts, including the conclusion that suffering isn't good for anything.

"What did you mean by being a woman in Hollywood?" I asked.

"Yes, enough about you, let's talk about me." She wiped her mouth with her napkin. "I'm a screenwriter. Or at least I was."

"You were?"

"You bet your boots."

"What movies did you write?"

"Did you ever see *Pretty Woman*?"

"Are you kidding? You wrote that?"

"You know the scene when Julia Roberts realizes that her childhood fantasy about a knight on a white horse is offensive, childish nonsense, and that if she wants her life to change, *she* has to change it, not just wait around for some entitled rich guy like Richard Gere to rescue her?"

I thought back. "Um, I guess so."

"No, you don't. Because it's not in the movie! I did a draft, but absolutely nothing I wrote ended up on the screen. It's just as well. They knew exactly what tripe the audience wanted to see back then. Speaking of which, what the hell was that whole *Twilight* thing about? I thought your generation was supposed to be so much less sexist than mine."

I hung my head in mock-shame. "I have no defense. But I do know we shouldn't be lightly forgiven. My generation is going to have to, like, end war if we truly want to atone for *Twilight*."

Vernie snorted. "I wrote some other movies too."

"Like what?"

Vernie named a couple of films I'd never heard of, and also one called *Borrowing Trouble*.

"I know that one!" I said. "But I haven't seen it."

"Don't bother. It wasn't what I wrote either. I love Hollywood, but it's a crazy place. And it was a different world back then for women. Or maybe not so different. Do you like movies?"

"Oh, yeah," I said. "I was in one once."

"You were?"

"*Attack of the Soul-Sucking Brain Zombies.*"

"Well, I absolutely love the title."

"Yeah, well, I was just an extra, but you can see me in the cafeteria scene. But like you said, don't bother. It's terrible. Not even direct-to-DVD, I don't think. Direct-to-Netflix."

Vernie nodded soberly. "Yes, that's the way it often goes. But that's not the point. Did you like it?"

"What?"

"Acting."

I thought back. "Not really. I mean, it was sort of fun, even though it was a weird time in my life. But acting isn't for me."

"Then it's a really good thing you did it."

"Why?"

"You found out you didn't like acting. How great is that?"

I hadn't really thought about it that way, but it did sort of make sense.

I took a sip of wine. We'd had cocktails before dinner and now wine with the food. I was just glad I'd taken the bus.

"So if not acting," Vernie said, "what do you wanna do with your life? What are your hopes and dreams?"

At that, I took *another* drink of wine. But it didn't help me answer the question.

"I'm not sure I have any," I said.

"Of course you do. What did you study in school?"

"Psychology and political science. They're okay. But mostly I chose them just to shut my parents up."

"Fantastic! That's two more things you can check off your list. What about your job?"

"Well, lifeguarding definitely isn't my dream. Although I'm glad I was doing it this week."

Vernie grinned.

"And I also work in a bakery, but, well, I hate it."

"You know what that means," Vernie said.

"Okay, yeah, but now that I know those things aren't my dream, how come I have to keep doing them?"

Vernie laughed. "Oh, you're *definitely* a whiskey sour. Don't worry. It'll all be clear in the end."

"I guess." I explained how envious I was of my friends Min and Gunnar for having Unstoppable Career Drive and Passionate Aimlessness when I didn't have either, and how it seemed like everyone around me was on one of those two tracks. Everyone except me.

Vernie leaned in closer. "I'll let you in on a little secret. It's not just your friends, and it's not just now. Those have always been the two choices in life, at least if you wanna be happy."

"So I'm never going to be happy?"

"Sure, you are," Vernie said. "It's like with your drink. Just because you don't know what your dream is, that doesn't mean you don't have one. It just means you haven't discovered it yet."

I didn't like the turn this conversation was taking. I'd finally found someone to tell me that there really *was* a secret to life, something that everyone else knew except me, but it was something stupid like, *The secret is different for everyone.* Or, *It's something you must discover on your own.* Fuck that. I wanted ANSWERS. Clear! Understandable! Answers! Was that really too much to ask?

"Russel?"

I looked up at her.

"I'm an old lady. You have to humor me on this, okay?"

I smiled. "Okay."

"I mean it. The fact that you don't know your dream? That's a *good* thing. That means it's a *good* dream. Dreams aren't like drinks—they're not as easy to pick, and they're harder to change. I was thirty before I realized I wanted to be a screenwriter."

"You were? Wow." At least I caught myself before I said, "That's *old!*"

We were mostly done with dinner now, so Vernie said, "Hold on, I'll be right back." Then she gathered up our plates and disappeared into the kitchen, returning a few minutes later with a little cake and candles.

"You didn't need to do that," I said.

"Of course I did. You saved my life! And remember, one day I'm going to pay you back by saving yours too."

And as she was slicing up the cake, I thought to myself, *Okay, Vernie definitely isn't Stifler's Mom, or Blanche Dubois, or even Kathy Griffin.*

She was better.

CHAPTER FIVE

For what it's worth, I couldn't stop thinking about Kevin. Which was really stupid. I mean, it was so blindingly obvious what it was all about: I was disappointed with my life, I'd run into my high school boyfriend who reminded me of the last time I'd been truly happy, and now I was stupidly assuming that if I was back together with him, I'd be happy again, just like before.

But it wasn't that easy. Life didn't work like that. I'd changed, he'd changed. You can't go home again, you never step in the same river twice, you can't reassemble the scrambled eggs.

The past is the past.

Still, I'd been thinking about this enough that I knew I had to talk to someone about it. I'd been too embarrassed to ask Min and Gunnar, "So what's the secret to life that everyone knows except me?" But I could ask them this. So a couple of days after my dinner with Vernie, I decided to talk to them about Kevin.

Gunnar was holed up in his bedroom on the computer, but Min and I were sitting up on the deck on the top of the houseboat, watching the sunset. The view from up there was ridiculously beautiful, with the sleek glass skyscrapers of downtown reflecting the orange glow of the sinking sun. All it needed was little CGI spaceships flying around, and it'd be a stunning futuristic paradise in some James Cameron movie. And you can literally see the Space Needle from there, which is just so cool, like moving to Hollywood and having a view of the "Hollywood" sign out your apartment window.

The houseboat rocked slightly, and water gurgled. On the lake in front of us, sailboats floated by. I always wondered who these people were, the folks out sailboating at eight o'clock on a Tuesday evening. How had they arranged their lives that they were able to not work and afford boats like that? More importantly, why were they not me?

Finally, I turned to Min. "Do you think I should call Kevin?"

"Yes," Min said.

"Really? You do?"

"Absolutely. Call him. You know you want to. And it's the right thing to do."

"I do want to," I said "But it just seems so pathetic. I mean, I dump him because I'm feeling pissy and ignored. Then three years later, after my life goes completely to shit, I go pathetically crawling back to him, saying, 'Please, Kevin, I was wrong, take me back.'"

"Your life hasn't gone to shit," she said. "You're being completely melodramatic as usual. But you should still call him."

"You really think so?" I said.

"Absolutely, without a doubt, no question."

I looked back toward downtown. The last few years, Seattle has sort of gone crazy—economically, I mean. Things may have been tough in the rest of the country, but not here. The whole South Lake Union area—the area between Lake Union and downtown—is being transformed. It used to be run-down warehouses and vacant lots, but they've cleared all that away. Now they're basically building a second downtown. Part of that is the new Amazon.com headquarters, which is supposed to include these three massive glass balls—each one big enough to fit a little park inside, with grass and trees and everything. I counted once, and I could literally see twenty-four different cranes just from the top of our houseboat. What would it all look like in five years when it was finally done?

Kevin's and my future was like that rising skyline—full of promise, full of optimism. Staring at it all, it was hard not to feel emboldened, to grab my phone and call him up and ask him to marry me right then and there.

"But what if he doesn't want to see me?" I said to Min.

Okay, so I didn't feel *that* emboldened.

But before Min could answer, there was a creak on the deck behind us. At first I thought it was Gunnar joining us from his bedroom at last. I turned around, a smile on my face.

It wasn't Gunnar. No, it was the Min-ions, Trai and Lena.

The smiled slipped from my face like the sun disappearing behind the Olympic Mountains.

"Oh!" Min said. "Hey." Her face had lit up, the exact opposite of mine.

"Gunnar let us in," Lena explained.

"Hey," I said to the two of them, and Lena *sort of* nodded.

They both pulled up chairs on the other side of Min, which was awkward and a little insulting, since Min and I had basically been centered in the middle of the deck.

"*So?*" Lena said to Min, all excited. "How'd it go with Kennedy? Did you get the extension?"

Something to do with their graduate program. And sure enough, Min filled them both in on all the drama.

I stayed up on the deck a little while after that, staring over at the darkening skyline, trying to pay attention to what they were saying, despite it being totally boring. Finally I left, and I'm not sure Min even realized I was gone.

As for Kevin, I didn't call him. But truthfully, for a while, even I wasn't sure why I didn't. Then it finally occurred to me: I was kind of *afraid* to contact him— even if I wasn't exactly sure what I was afraid *of.* That we'd get back together and I'd still be frustrated and unhappy? Then I'd have to accept that the problem with my life wasn't my lack of Kevin at all—that the problem was *me.*

I guess on some level I sort of liked the idea that Kevin was out there somewhere, just waiting to step in and solve all my problems and make my life wonderful. The minute I actually saw him again, all that went away. It really was like that South Lake

Union skyline. It was full of promise as long as it was all scaffolding and cranes, but what happened when the buildings were finally done? What if they were ugly? What if they didn't fit well together? What if Amazon's celebrated geodesic balls turned out to be big ugly lumps? I didn't want Kevin's and my relationship to have lumpy balls! (Okay, that came out wrong, but you know what I mean.)

So almost a week went by, and pretty much nothing happened except work, sleep, and the occasional Xbox game. I knew life wasn't like *Pretty Woman*, where you only have to wish hard enough for a hot guy in a white limousine to come and solve all your problems (at least if you're pretty, which, let's face it, is basically the message of that movie). No, real life is like Vernie's alternate, un-filmed version of *Pretty Woman*, where nothing changes in your life until *you* change it.

But then came a day I was working at Bake again.

"I can't believe you let this happen," Amanda was saying to Jake. "You *knew* the ad was running this week."

"Why is it my responsibility?" Jake said. "You knew the ad was running too."

Bake had placed its first-ever ad in the *Northwest Asian Weekly*, which is a local newspaper for the Asian community. We'd even started to get a few new customers too, which made sense since it was a community that (a) had a lot of money and (b) sometimes bought into weird, pop-culture-y trends like custom-baking your own loaf of bread. (Or is that racist? Seriously, you can tell me. I want to know.)

Problem is, we'd quickly run out of dried lychees. It wasn't a popular "integrant" in the first place—I could only remember three people ever wanting it in their bread. But Jake and Amanda were freaking out that Asian people were going to come into the store, see that we had no dried lychees, and run away screaming.

"I'll just go," Jake was saying. "I'll be right back."

"You *won't* be right back," Amanda said. "Uwajimaya is all the way on the other side of town!" This is Seattle's biggest (and best) Asian supermarket, located in the International District, and it was a pretty crazy drive, especially with the afternoon rush hour looming. "We'll go tonight after we close."

"*You'll* go tonight after work. I have to see my dad."

"You just saw your dad last weekend."

"For ten minutes," Jake said. "Besides, he needs a phone installed in his bathroom."

"He doesn't need a phone in the bathroom."

"Yes, he does. It's a safety thing. If he knocks the phone off the cradle, the switch board immediately calls the emergency crew."

"I'll go," I said.

"Why does he need a phone?" Amanda said to Jake, ignoring me. "He wears that button-thing around his neck."

"Which he always forgets in the bedroom. Which is why I'm installing the phone in the *bathroom*."

"I'll go!" I said, louder.

Jack and Amanda both looked at me.

"To Uwajimaya," I said. "I mean, if you need someone to go, I don't mind. I'd just need to borrow your car."

In the end, they decided that, yes, having me go was best, even if it meant another fifteen-minute fight between Jake and Amanda over whether or not I was covered by their insurance.

Uwajimaya is simply fantastic. If you take a quick scan, it mostly looks just like any other American super-market—big and bright and colorful. But if you look closer, you realize that everything is actually different. Some things are *very* different. For example, the sea-food section has a big tank full of live octopi. And there are fish heads, and massive geoduck clams, and a zillion different kinds of live crab. Elsewhere in the store, there's a whole aisle devoted to nothing but dried noodles. And they must stock forty different kinds of soy sauce, and at least twenty kinds of nori.

Best of all, most of the food is shipped directly from Asia, so the labels don't bother with English at all. Want to know what's in your miso soup mix and you don't read Japanese? Then you're in the wrong store. And if you're grossed out by things like boiled silkworm larvae, well, you really need to get out more.

I'd been to Uwajimaya a million times, so it didn't take me long to find the dried lychee nuts. But Jake and Amanda didn't know that, so I took my own sweet time.

I explored the produce. With a name like dragon fruit, it had to be good, right?

I examined the electric tea pots. It reminded me how Min was always saying her parents are total snobs about tea, even though she's a total tea snob herself. Snobbery, like beauty, is totally in the eye of the beholder.

Finally, I considered going upstairs to check out the cookbooks, despite the fact that none of them are written in English.

And then, standing in the middle of the massive fresh sushi section, I saw Kevin.

I literally caught my breath. I'd never done that before, so I didn't even know what it felt like (a cross between a gulp and a choke).

He wasn't riding in a white limousine like Richard Gere in *Pretty Woman*, but it didn't matter. I was flooded with feelings of affection—I was drowning in a whole goddamn lake of them.

I was watching him, but he didn't see me, just like before. But this time he was barely ten feet away, and there was no crowd for him to get lost into. In other words, there was no chance of him getting away.

Do I even have time to talk to him? I actually had to think about that. With iPhone technology constantly changing, I had to seriously consider: were there any possible apps that Jake and Amanda could use to track me and realize I was goofing off?

More importantly, do I want to talk to him? Once we talked, I'd have to accept whatever came next. Like, if his reappearance in my life didn't make everything wonderful again.

Truthfully, that kind of nonsense was a lot easier to accept when Kevin was mostly in the abstract, not when he was standing right in front of me with his neatly trimmed black beard. That was something new—he hadn't had a beard before. He filled out his shirt more now, and his pants too, but both in very good ways. And he hadn't worn glasses before either.

But even so, I couldn't make myself walk over to

him. My pulse was pounding, but the blood didn't seem to be going anywhere. The warm feeling suddenly turned cold. I was remembering our break-up, how petty it was, what a dick I'd been. Would he remember that? Would he hold it against me?

I turned to leave.

At the same time, he turned toward me.

"Russel?" he said.

I looked back.

His face was warm and friendly and open. He was drowning in all the same feelings I'd been having only a few seconds earlier—I could tell. He hadn't remembered why or how we'd broken up, what a dick I'd been. Or maybe he did, but it paled compared to everything else he felt about me.

"Kevin?" I said, acting surprised, like I hadn't just been watching him for three minutes straight.

"How *are* you?"

He really *was* happy to see me. His face was blossoming like a flower.

"I'm good," I said.

He stepped toward me, and I stepped toward him. We hugged, loosely, a little awkwardly. He had absolutely filled out, and it was definitely in a good way. I think he was wearing cologne, but I didn't get a good sense of it, or of his own scent, over all the crazy smells of the store.

He pulled back from the hug first, then I pulled back.

"It's funny," I said. "I saw you a couple of weeks ago. Out at U Village. But I lost you in the crowd."

"You did? Huh, I don't remember—oh, yeah, I met some friends for dinner."

I nodded. "So you're living in Seattle now?"

"I am. I moved back just a couple of months ago. I work for Amazon."

"Oh, God, don't tell me you're a 'brogrammer'!" There were two kinds of guys who worked in tech in Seattle: geeks and "brogrammers"—basically, jocky frat-type guys who've realized that tech is where the big bucks are. And it went without saying that Kevin was no geek.

Kevin laughed. "No, not tech. I actually work for IMDb—they're owned by Amazon. Editing."

"Kevin Land is an editor, huh? Who knew?"

"Turns out there's hope for us dumb jocks after all. What about you? What do you do?"

I told him about my two jobs. When it came to winning him back, I wasn't sure which was the better strategy: puffing up the jobs to make them sound more impressive than they were, or making them sound really pathetic and I was a complete lost wet puppy in need of rescuing. I couldn't decide, so I just told him the truth (which, unfortunately, was closer to "lost wet puppy in need of rescuing").

Kevin listened and smiled. He'd whitened his teeth at some point in the last three years—probably professionally, in a dentist's office, not with those stupid Crest Strips that I'd used (that had barely made any difference I could see).

When I told him about how I'd rescued Vernie, he said, "You actually saved someone's life? I'm impressed. Can't say I've ever done anything like that before."

You saved my *life*, I wanted to say. *Back in high school. Before I met you, I was this scared, lonely little boy. But in the end, you made me feel like a man. You made me feel loved and sexy and important for the first—and only—time in my life.*

And maybe, if things go according to plan, you can do all that for me all over again.

"Meh," I said. "It wasn't any big deal."

"It is!" he said. "It really is."

And I was so pleased that Kevin was impressed that I smiled. (But then I remembered how yellow my teeth were compared to Kevin's, so I closed my mouth again.)

"It's pretty great, isn't it?" Kevin said.

"What?" I said.

"I don't know. Seattle in the summer. Being out of college. Life. Everyone says the future is shit, but it doesn't feel that way. Does it?"

"No, it doesn't," I said, and I was mostly telling the truth again, even if the only reason the future felt bright to me right then was because I was starting to think there was a real chance that Kevin and I would get back together again.

"I feel bad," I said.

"For what?"

"The way we broke up."

Kevin looked confused.

"Remember? I was mad because you didn't come home for vacation? So I refused to talk to you?"

He smiled—more of those white teeth. "That's not the way I remember it."

"It isn't?" I smiled too—yellow teeth be damned.

He shook his head.

"Well, I'm sorry anyway."

"Russel, you don't have anything to apologize for. That was a long time ago. It's all good. I think of you all the time, and I only ever think good thoughts. In fact, I've been meaning to contact you."

"Really?" Needless to say, my heart was singing.

And a chorus of angels was joining in, all perfectly in tune.

He nodded—forcefully. "Yeah."

"Because I was just wondering..."

"Yeah?" he said.

"Well, we both live in Seattle now. I was wondering if maybe you wanna go out with me sometime."

Kevin's white teeth disappeared. Which meant his smile did too.

"Oh, Russel."

"What?" I said. Had the light in this store always been so bright? Had the floor always been this sticky?

"I'm really sorry."

"About what?"

"I have a boyfriend."

"You have..." At that, a massive meteor slammed into the Earth, totally wiping out me, Uwajimaya, and the entire chorus of angels. Or maybe a sinkhole opened under my feet and I fell down into it, all the way to the planet's molten core. I wasn't sure which it was, but it didn't matter, because I couldn't feel anything anyway.

Of course Kevin has a boyfriend. People who looked like he did, people who were positive and optimistic about the future, they always had boyfriends, at least if they wanted them.

"We live together," Kevin said. "I should've mentioned him right away. That was so stupid. I don't know why I didn't. I didn't mean to lead you on. I thought you were with someone too. Weren't you seeing someone?"

"Sort of," I said. "But it didn't last." That had been two years ago, and it hadn't been anything serious anyway.

"Well, it's only a matter of time. Assuming that's what you want. I mean, maybe you're happy being single." He swatted at the air. "I'm sorry, that was a stupid thing to say. I know you want a relationship. Geez, I'm an idiot, aren't I?"

I shook my head. "It's fine. It was just a misunderstanding. So you're living with someone, huh? What's he like?"

"He's good. He's great. But you don't want to hear about him."

"No, I guess not," I said. "I should get back. I mean, I'm technically working now."

"Yeah, okay. I understand. But Russel?"

I stopped.

"I really would like to be friends. Real friends, I mean. I totally understand if you don't want to. But you're an important part of my life, and we live in the same city now, and, well, I'd love to try to be friends if you do."

This was a serious decision. Did I want to be "friends" with Kevin Land? After all, I'd spent the last few weeks convincing myself he was the solution to all my problems—that if we ended up back together, I could recapture the passion and magic of my youth. But that wasn't going to happen now. So wouldn't being friends with him be like a seal trying to make friends with a shark? It would have been one thing if Kevin was happy in his life and I was happy in my own life. Or if I was happy and Kevin was unhappy. But Kevin being happy and me being unhappy had disaster written all over it.

So of course I smiled my biggest smile, even showing him my yellow teeth, and said, "Of course! I absolutely want to be friends."

* * *

Boston's apartment still smelled like dust and old kitchen grease.

That day after work, I'd texted him, the guy I'd had that hook-up with before. I'd asked if he wanted to get together again, and he'd said yes, so I'd come directly from work. Looking around his apartment, it occurred to me: this was probably the kind of place I'd be living in if I hadn't had a rich friend like Gunnar to sponge off of.

Why had I come here? It wasn't (just) that I was horny. It was that thing with Kevin, seeing him in Uwajimaya. It had really screwed with my mind, exactly like I'd been worried it would. Talk about tearing the paper lantern off the light bulb!

I'd wanted someone to talk to about Kevin again, but Gunnar and Min had both seemed so distracted lately. Plus, I guess I wanted a "gay" perspective.

Oh, and I *was* horny. There's that too.

"*Rustler!*" Boston said as I stood in the doorway. This was kind of fun. I'd only met him that one time before, and he already had a nickname for me.

I smiled. "Thanks for inviting me over."

"Sure, come on in."

He was wearing navy blue cotton pants and a light blue short-sleeve shirt with the words "Al's Auto" embroidered on the breast. He was leaner than Kevin, but had good lines.

"You're a mechanic?" I said.

"Yup, I'm a grease monkey." He held up his hands to show the actual car oil on them, but I resisted making the obvious "lube" joke. "Does that turn you on?" he said.

"Yeah, kinda," I said. I nodded down at my white "Bake" shirt. "I work at a bakery. That turn *you* on?"

He laughed at my joke, which made me feel a little tiny bit better.

"Wanna fuck?" he said.

"Yeah," I said, but when he started for the bedroom, I lingered in the main room. I guess that right then, I wanted to talk more than I wanted to fuck. Who knew?

Boston returned and puppy-dog-faced me. "'Sup, Rustler?"

"I just ran into my old boyfriend. From high school. He has a new boyfriend now."

"Ohhh, man." Somehow sensing that this was more than an anecdote, he turned for refrigerator and pulled out a couple of beers. He held one toward me.

I took it. After we popped the tops, we sank down onto his couch.

"It's funny," I said. "I saw him a couple of weeks ago, so I knew he was living in Seattle now." Then I explained how I'd worked it out in my head that if I could get back together with Kevin, all my current problems and frustrations would somehow go away. And how even at the time, I'd known it was stupid, so I'd avoided calling him, just to keep the fantasy alive. But now the fantasy was dead and cremated and the ashes were scattered across all seven continents, and I felt like absolute shit about it.

"I *totally* get that," Boston said. "I really, really do."

And just for the record? If it seems strange that I'd gone over to a guy's apartment for cheap hook-up sex and ended up talking about how I was still in love with my ex-boyfriend, then you've never had a fuck buddy before. Not that I've had a whole lot of them—or any of them, really. In fact, seeing Boston for a second time, that was the closest I'd ever come to a fuck buddy in my life. But I'm gay in Seattle in 2014, so I know how the concept works. The whole point is that it *isn't* a romantic relationship. Everyone is very clear right from the start. You're literally friends who sometimes have sex, and unlike in the movies, it's not confusing at all. So when one person talks about how they've just been devastated by an ex-boyfriend, the other person acts like a friend, not like someone you intend to be rolling around with, naked and sweaty, in just a few minutes.

If you live in a city and you're under the age of thirty, you already know all the pros and cons of fuck buddies. But right then, being with Boston and having him listen to me even as I knew I'd be kissing and holding him a few minutes later, it felt a little bit like the next step in human evolution.

Sure enough, Boston told me how he'd been crushing on one of his mechanic co-workers for months, even though he knew the guy was totally straight. (He even showed me a picture, and the guy was definitely hot.) He told me how the guy had spent the night at his place once, and he'd had an actual opportunity to make a move. But he didn't do it, and not just because he didn't want to come across as creepy or anything. He didn't want to ruin the fantasy that one day he and this guy would be together—not because of some drunken, late-night romp, but actually *together*. Boston said he knew it would probably never happen. But he was living on the .001% chance that it might, that the guy secretly loved him back, and in the end they'd be together. He clung to it like a barnacle to a rock in the ocean.

In other words, Boston may have been a self-proclaimed grease monkey, but he really did know exactly what I was a going through. It made me feel better, knowing that I wasn't the only one who felt stuff like this—that other people went through things like this too.

"But now it's too late for me," I said. "I know the truth. So what do I do?"

Boston leaned back against the couch and thought for a second. He took a swig of beer, then said, "Fuck him. Forget it and move on."

It wasn't the worst advice in the world. But it was also easier said than done.

"Don't take it all so seriously. Everything'll work out in the end."

He was being annoyingly *hakuna matata* all of a sudden, but he was still right about this too.

"And in the meantime, let's fuck!"

He stood up from the couch, and I could already see the bulge in his navy blue cotton pants. I wasn't kidding before when I'd said that his being a mechanic was a turn-on. It was also his whole casual, carefree attitude—because, if you haven't realized it by now, that is just so. Not. Me.

He popped the top button on his pants—he was wearing blue and green plaid boxers, which was actually very sexy, mostly because they reminded me that he was this butch mechanic—and started sauntering toward the bedroom, his pants sliding farther down as he walked.

"Come on," he said. "We can bareback now."

I stopped again. "What?"

He looked back at me. "Huh? Oh, yeah, I'm on PrEP. Been seven days now too."

This was this new-ish pill—I could never remember exactly what it stands for. But basically the idea is that HIV-negative people go on lower-level HIV medications, and then your chance of getting infected is really low—at least if you take the pill every single day. It's a little like the pill women take to not get pregnant, except it's a thousand times more expensive. The latest word was that every guy who is at any risk for HIV at all should take the drug (at least if their insurance pays for it). I'd been meaning to see my doctor about it too.

"That doesn't mean you can bareback," I said. That basically means having sex without condoms. Full sex. *Penetrative* sex.

"Sure, it does."

"No, no. You're still supposed to use condoms, at least with people you don't absolutely know are HIV-negative. Like, after being monogamous and getting tested together?"

Boston looked at me, his face completely blank.

"PrEP lowers your chance of getting HIV, but it doesn't eliminate it completely," I said. "Besides, there are other diseases."

"I slammed my dick in a car door once," Boston said. "But I was wearing a condom at the time, so I didn't feel a thing."

It took me a second to realize that he was making a joke about the fact that condoms cut down on the feeling of sex. But what had made Boston think that I'd be willing to have unprotected sex with him— even if he really *was* on PrEP? We hadn't literally "fucked" the last time I'd been here. I'd *never* fucked with a random hook-up. The last time I'd been here, Boston had sucked my dick, and I'd corn-cobbed his.

But mostly we'd just kissed and thrust together and jerked each other off until we'd both come.

Finally, Boston said, "I don't get it. What's the problem?"

"Well, for one thing, what if you're lying?"

"I'm not."

"But how do I know that?"

"I dunno. I guess you should be on PrEP too."

"That's not the point."

"What the point?"

"The point," I said, "is that life isn't a Sean Cody video."

The expression on his face was still completely blank. And the bulge in his pants was exactly as big as before.

I realized I didn't know Boston at all, that we had barely anything in common. Why would we? It had just been a random hook-up.

"I think I'm gonna go," I said.

"What?" he said. It was like my words literally made no sense.

"This just feels wrong."

"We don't have to fuck," he said. "Not if you don't want to. We can do whatever you want."

I'd like to say that I shook my head no and just walked out the door.

But I didn't. I followed Boston into the bedroom, and we stripped and rolled around naked for a while, exactly like before.

For about five minutes, it helped me forget Kevin. But then after I left, I think I felt even worse than before, even more lonely.

Fuck buddies was an interesting idea, but now I

was thinking that maybe it wasn't the next step in human evolution after all.

CHAPTER SIX

A couple of days later, I was in my room in the houseboat poking around online, and I heard this weird thumping from somewhere down below. I figured either we were being robbed, or we were being attacked by the giant squid from *20,000 Leagues Under the Sea*.

Turns out it was Gunnar, futzing around in the houseboat's one non-bedroom closet storage area, under the stairs. (The problem with having only one storage area isn't just the lack of storage space—it's also the fact that if you want anything at all out of storage, you basically have to take everything out, sort through it, then put it all back in again.)

Gunnar had already put his backpack off to one side of the hall.

"What's up?" I said.

"I'm going on a hike," he said. He peered into some half-collapsed cardboard boxes.

"Yeah?" I said. "When? Where?"

"Today. Now." He pulled a collapsible tent from one of the boxes. "It's sort of this Bigfoot thing."

"Whoa. Really?" It was already, like, noon. "With who exactly?"

"These people I met online. They're some of the preeminent Bigfoot researchers in the world." He found his down sleeping bag. "You wanna come?"

I had to think about this. I did have the day off—and I was pretty sure I could swap some shifts and get the next day off too. I could go if we were back early-ish the day after. Besides, who wouldn't want to go on a search for Bigfoot? If I didn't have any passions or drives of my own, maybe I could at least borrow Gunnar's for a few days.

Between the two of us, we quickly managed to cobble together enough equipment and supplies for a couple of nights in the woods. Mostly, I was just happy to be getting away from my own pathetic life for a bit.

We headed north out of town toward Highway 2, which takes Stevens Pass over the Cascade Mountains.

As we drove, I said, "So you really think Bigfoot might be real?"

"I think it's possible," he said.

"Min doesn't think so. She says it's unscientific."

"It's never unscientific to ask the question."

I thought about this. This was Gunnar's latest project, and I was determined to keep an open mind, but still. "How is it different from asking if Santa Claus is real?"

"There's no evidence Santa Claus exists," Gunnar said. "With Bigfoot, there's at least eyewitness accounts. And *some* forensic evidence."

"Forensic evidence?"

"Hair. Footprints. Scat."

"In that case, it's probably a good thing there's no forensic evidence of Santa Claus!"

I laughed, but Gunnar didn't.

"You know," I said. "Santa comes down the chimney and takes a shit in your living room?"

Gunnar still didn't laugh, just kept driving and staring straight ahead, which annoyed me a little. I thought my joke was pretty funny.

"In 2013, a group of scientists did the first serious study of the Yeti, or Abominable Snowman," Gunnar said. "They did DNA analysis of thirty-six different samples of hair that were said to be from the creature. They matched the DNA with all the samples in the GenBank, the world's largest collection of DNA. Most of the hair came back as being from horses or bears or wolves. But two of the samples came back as perfect matches for an extinct species of prehistoric polar bear."

As he gripped the steering wheel, Gunnar glanced over at me. Clearly he expected me to be impressed.

"Okay," I said. "So?"

"Don't you see? For one thing, polar bears don't live in the Himalayas. For another thing, this was an extinct species."

"But the Abominable Snowman isn't supposed to be a bear. Is it? I thought it was supposed to be a great ape, like Bigfoot."

"You're missing the point. There's now scientific evidence that there's an unknown, thought-to-be extinct species of bear living in the Himalayas! And being a polar bear, this bear would be much more aggressive than the other bears there, just like the legend of the Abominable Snowman says."

I still didn't say anything. I wasn't sure what I was supposed *to* say.

"Don't you see?" Now Gunnar sounded annoyed. "It looks like the Abominable Snowman was based on something real. It's not just a myth or a legend."

"Ah. So Bigfoot might be based on something real too?"

"Yes!" Gunnar was happy that I was finally getting the point, even if he was exasperated it had taken me so long to see it.

"So have they done this kind of DNA analysis on the forensic evidence they have of Bigfoot?" I said.

Gunnar didn't say anything for a second, just kept clenching the steering wheel and staring straight ahead. "That doesn't mean anything. Most of the samples from the Abominable Snowman study came back negative too."

An hour or so later, we finally crossed over the pass and started heading down into the foothills on the other side of the mountains.

"So where are we going anyway?" I asked. Gunnar and I hadn't spoken much since I'd pissed him off with my Bigfoot push-back, but I didn't want the whole trip to feel awkward.

"It's a tributary of Nason Creek," he said.

That didn't mean a damn thing to me, but I nodded as if it did.

We drove on in silence again. The wind whistled through a gap in my window. One thing I really liked about Gunnar was that he hadn't blown a lot of his money on an expensive new car. It was a red Geo Prizm from the 1990s, and both the radio and the air conditioning had long since stopped working.

But then we took a turn off the main highway, and I started to worry about that car of his. It was all national forest, so there were no houses or farms, and my cell phone coverage had dropped long ago, out along Highway 2. What happened if we had car trouble?

"Who are these people exactly?" I said. "The ones we're meeting." I felt kind of stupid that I was only asking this now.

"They're just people I've been chatting with online," he said. "Once they saw I was really serious about this Bigfoot thing, that I wasn't just another weekend warrior, they've been really helpful."

I couldn't help but think that maybe what they were attracted to was Gunnar's money. It wouldn't be hard to discover that he was a twenty-three-year-old almost-millionaire. The story had been all over the internet a few years back.

"Right now they're trying to raise money to build a Bigfoot blimp," he said.

"A what?"

"It's a remote-controlled blimp. It's really the perfect way to search for Bigfoot. There's too much territory to search on foot, and helicopters and planes are too loud. They can build it for a quarter million dollars."

And here we go, I thought.

"I know what you're thinking," Gunnar said.

"Oh?" I said.

"Why not a drone?"

"Um, yeah, okay," I said. "Why *not* a drone?"

"Also too loud. If we know anything about Bigfoot, it's that they're incredibly shy and elusive. They'd have to be to avoid detection all these years. A small, un-manned blimp with thermal imaging is the perfect way to observe them, especially at night, since they're probably nocturnal."

"Right," I said.

We drove in silence a little longer. The car bounced and skittered on the gravel road. When had the road turned to gravel? I hadn't even noticed.

"Gunnar—" I started to say.

"They haven't asked me for money," he said. "And I wouldn't give it to them if they did. I'm not stupid. They're doing a Kickstarter campaign. I might contribute to that, but only, you know, maybe a hundred dollars or so."

"That's cool," I said. "Maybe I'll contribute too."

We took a few more side roads, and drove for another hour or so, before we finally arrived at the campground. Except it wasn't a campground. It was just a row of old cars parked along the side of the road. Gunnar and I parked our car behind the others.

"How do we know these are the right people?" I said.

Gunnar nodded to a nearby bumper sticker: *I brake for Sasquatch!*

Really? I wanted to say. This was his confirmation?

We worked our way through the trees. There was a

gully next to the road, and a small stream running down through it. The water fizzed and gurgled around the deadfall in the water—wood that had been stripped of its bark and bleached white like driftwood on a beach. At some point during the year, this thing flooded bad. But it was late June, and the flooding was already done for the year, right?

There was a cluster of blue and red tents set up on a grassy bank next to the creek. There were people too, three men and a woman, mostly in jeans and flannel, and all of them in heavy boots. The second we cleared the trees, they looked over at us, one by one. One guy was down on his haunches, fiddling with the campfire. As we approached, he stood up, eyes on us. But we'd been driving for hours, and the sun was now low in the sky, farther down the creek valley, which meant they were all in silhouette, their faces in shadow. Were they happy to see us—or angry that we'd invaded their campsite? Were these even the people Gunnar had come to meet? Without seeing their faces, how could he tell?

But Gunnar headed forward, and I followed sheepishly behind, my over-stuffed backpack squeaking on my shoulders.

"You must be Gunnar," one of the men said when we were closer.

You must be Gunnar? I thought. Was it really possible that we'd driven all this way, deep into a remote forest, to meet up with a group of people Gunnar had never even met in person? And before he'd invited me to join him, he'd been planning to do that *alone*? (On the other hand, how was this different from meeting someone for an online hook-up?)

"Ben?" Gunnar said.

"That's me," the man said.

The shadows fell away, and the four faces were revealed at last.

Four friendly faces.

They were old, in their forties maybe. Their hair was tousled, and the men all had beards, but they were mostly trimmed. They had good posture too. Basically, they were a cross between "mountain man" and "beloved community college professor." One of them was black, and I thought, *Cool, a Bigfoot hunter of color.* Which is probably totally racist, but it's still not something you see every day.

And the men were actually pretty hot, especially Ben. I'd never been particularly attracted to old guys, but there was something about this guy's open-faced smile. His hair and beard weren't quite brown and they weren't quite golden—they were more the color of a perfectly toasted marshmallow. Leon was tall and lean and boyish with straight jet black hair, and Clive, the African American guy, had the thickest body, but he mostly looked solid, not fat. Meanwhile, Katie, the woman, was blond and fit, like a middle-aged mom in an ad for granola bars.

I guess hunting for Bigfoot kept a person in pretty good shape.

When Gunnar had finished introducing me, Clive said, "You guys were coming from Seattle, right?"

"Yeah," I said.

"We had a *great* day today," Ben said. "We were out at the viewing site, and I think we even found a partial footprint. After dinner, I'll show you our cast."

"Oh, no!" Katie said, and we all turned to look at her. She was crouched down, looking into a cooler. "I brought a left-over ice cream cake for dessert, but it's melting fast. Oh, well, I guess we'll just have to have dessert first."

So that's exactly what we did, even before Gunnar and I had a chance to set up our tent: we had half-melted ice cream cake sitting around the campfire on the bank of that little tributary to Nason Creek, watching the sun sink the rest of the way behind the trees.

"You have to give Bigfoot credit," Leon said. "He knows the best places to hang out."

He wasn't kidding. That little gully was beautiful, like one of those secret places you read about in books that you have to go through some kind of magical gateway to get to, out of place and time. The air smelled of pine and running water, and a purple fog of campfire smoke swirled and twitched in the air above the creek.

After dessert, Gunnar and I set up our tent while Ben and Katie (who were married) finished cooking dinner, which turned out to be Cornish game hens stuffed with carrots and herbed rice. Each one was wrapped in tinfoil and cooked directly in the embers. And if dessert had been good, the main course was even better.

"This is incredible," I said, meaning the game hens. "What's your secret?"

"They say that everything tastes better around a campfire," Katie said, and we all sort of nodded. Then she added, "But you know who says that? *Jealous cooks!*"

We all laughed.

After dinner, well after the sun had set, we sat around the campfire again. I was sort of expecting to spend the evening debating the existence of Bigfoot (and after listening to Gunnar these last few weeks, I was already sort of dreading it). I at least expected them to talk more about their trip to the viewing site that afternoon. Hadn't they said they were going to show us the plaster cast they'd made of that partial Bigfoot print?

But to my surprise, Ben and the others mostly talked about their kids and things like kitchen remodels. Ben and Katie were Microsoft million-aires—they'd worked there during the nineties boom, then cashed in their stock options and retired early. Clive really was a college professor, and Leon was a high school librarian.

At one point, Clive said, "Remember the expedition to Lookout Mountain? Man, what a horrible climb."

"Oh, yeah," Ben said. "But it sure was worth it."

Why? I thought. Had they seen Bigfoot? But they didn't go into any detail about that trip either, just went off on a story about how Ben, Katie, and their daughter had once climbed Mount Kilimanjaro. No one even mentioned the Bigfoot blimp, which I was actually sort of curious about. Maybe Bigfoot never came up because they all spent so much time talking about it online, and also because they all already *believed* in Bigfoot, so there wasn't really any point in rehashing the evidence, and they didn't feel the need to convince skeptical listeners like me.

Weirdly, the more the group didn't talk about Bigfoot, the more I wanted to know what they had to say. So finally, when the fire had died down to sputtering embers, I just asked.

"Have any of you ever actually *seen* Bigfoot?"

They all exchanged glances over the flames. Ben puffed on a cigar. Gunnar looked over at me, and I wondered if I'd embarrassed him. Maybe that was a question you weren't supposed to ask, like a straight person asking a gay guy if he's a top or a bottom.

But then Ben exhaled a cloud of smoke. It flowed into the smoke from the campfire. The embers whined.

"I was fourteen years old," he said. "My family and I had gone up to Stehekin, the little town at the very end of Lake Chelan. The only way you could get there was by ferry all the way up the lake, and that's still the only way to get there short of hiking in. We were staying in this little cabin, and for some reason I woke up really early. I went out to use the outhouse. It was just barely light out, and the whole world was crisp and clean and green. When I opened the door to walk back from the outhouse, there was a deer right outside. It stared at me, and I stared at it for a long time. Like, ten minutes. I actually sat down in the grass, and neither of us moved. It finally wandered away, and I stood up and started to walk away. And right in front of me, watching me exactly the way I'd been watching the deer was this thing—covered with hair, standing upright. I looked right into its eyes, and I just knew that it was intelligent, like it was human. It definitely wasn't a bear or an elk or a deer. But it never even occurred to me that it might be a person. It was intelligent, but it wasn't human. It wasn't scared, and I wasn't scared either. It was exactly like it had been with that deer—I felt this connection. And after a couple minutes, it turned and just walked into the woods."

(Side-note? It was actually fun to listen to Ben go on like this, because let's face it: he was kind of dreamy, and his talking gave me a chance to stare openly.)

"At that point, it was like a storm broke in my head," Ben went on, "and I went inside all excited and shouting, waking up my family. And they went out to see, but by then it was gone. So of course they all said that I'd dreamt it. They were so certain that I must have been sleeping, that I'd mixed up a dream with reality, that after a while I started to think they were right—that I really *had* dreamt it all. It wasn't until about an hour later that I realized that it might've left tracks. And so I went to where I'd seen it, and sure enough, there were tracks."

"Did you show them to your family?" I said.

"I thought about it. But I knew they'd think I made them myself. So I didn't say anything. And ever since then..."

"You've spent your life looking for Bigfoot, trying to get another look."

"Pretty much."

At that, we all fell silent again, staring at the fire.

I have no idea what Ben actually saw all those years ago, but I knew in my bones that he wasn't lying to me, that he absolutely believed what he was telling me was the truth.

That night, outside Gunnar's and my tent, things fluttered and skittered and hooted and scratched. At one point, something even huffed like a horse. It was like a joke how much stuff was going on. And yet, when I stuck my head out the flap of our tent, all I saw was a few insects swirling in the light of my flashlight. It was no wonder that human beings have always been so quick to trap and prune and zap and kill nature. It was unnerving.

And then there was the matter of Bigfoot itself. It occurred to me that even the most hardened Bigfoot skeptic, even Min, might at least reconsider her beliefs while lying in a flimsy tent in an area where the creature had recently been spotted. And then there was the question of bears, which I knew for a fact lived in the area—or maybe extinct polar bears that didn't turn out to be extinct after all.

"Gunnar?" I said.

"Yeah?" he said, lying next to me in the tent.

"You said that Bigfoot are nocturnal, right?"

"Probably."

"What does that mean exactly?"

"Are you worried about one of them attacking us?"

"Would you think I'm an idiot if I said yes?"

Even in the dark, I could tell he was smiling.

"Well, if that happened," he said, "we would be the first recorded case of a Bigfoot attacking a human in the history of the world."

That was definitely reassuring. On the other hand, I couldn't help but note the little tone of glee in Gunnar's voice, almost like, on some level, he'd actually be happy about it.

Gunnar was up early the next morning, raring to go even before the sun had come up. It took the others a little bit longer to get ready. Okay, a *lot* longer. Ben cooked a rousing breakfast, Clive and Katie did some fishing in the creek, and Leon checked the images on his motion-activated wildlife camera from the night before (he didn't find anything interesting, which was surprising given that I'd personally heard a whole herd of mastodons pass by).

One bad thing about this impetuously-decided Bigfoot expedition into the woods? There was no outhouse in the vicinity. Which meant shitting in the woods like a bear.

Finally, around nine-thirty, we were all ready to go, which was a good thing, because Gunnar's head was on the verge of exploding.

We set off on a trail along the stream. Twigs and sticks crunched under our feet, and I realized I was the only one wearing tennis shoes. My feet slid on the slick carpet of pine needles.

"Is it far?" Gunnar asked Ben.

"Not too bad," Ben said.

"Who was it?" I asked. "What'd they see?"

"Three men out fishing," he said. "They'd been working their way upstream. One said he'd had the feeling all afternoon they were being watched. Then two of them rounded a bend, and there was the creature standing on the shore, watching them. That was three days ago. I'm just glad they had the foresight to mark it on their map."

We walked on for a bit, then I said, "So do you guys investigate everything that gets reported to you?"

"No. We do if they're accessible. But sometimes the best sightings are in the most remote areas. Loggers sometimes see incredible stuff. But we're just not equipped to do those kinds of backcountry expeditions. Not until we get the blimp built."

"How is that going?" I said, meaning the Kick-starter campaign.

Ben sighed. "Not so good. I don't understand it. We were on *Huffington Post* and everything."

At that, Ben stopped to consult his compass and a map. A few minutes later, we veered away from the stream, onto a different trail. That surprised me, since Ben had said that the site had been right along the creek.

Before long, I smelled sulfur. Now there was an even smaller stream on our left—a tributary to a tributary, I guess. And it looked like it was steaming.

"Are there hot springs around here?" I said.

"Just ahead," Clive said with a grin.

Sure enough, we came upon this pool nestled in the ferns, maybe ten feet across. Someone had encircled it with rocks, and there was a littering of trash too—all evidence that plenty of people had been here before. The water steamed and bubbled ever-so-slightly.

"I read about it online," Ben said. He smiled, even as he started unbuttoning his shirt. "What a coincidence, huh?" Suddenly the Bigfoot hunters were breaking out towels and undressing on every side of me.

"Wait," I said. "We're getting in?"

"Why not?" Katie said. "Now everyone turn around, please."

We all turned around, so Katie could finish undressing and slip into the water in private.

But the rest of us? We were just five guys. And only one of those guys—Gunnar—knew I was gay. And now the others (except for Gunnar) were shamelessly undressing all around me.

Shirts were shucked, and zippers slid down, showing boxers (on Leon and Clive) and boxer briefs (on Ben). Their bodies were furry, every one of them. They weren't like a lot of gay guys, pruned and shaved and trimmed. They'd all let their body hair grow completely wild (which, alas, also meant back hair, but what can you do?).

And then the undies were shucked, and the hair around me became thicker, denser, even more wild. Between their legs, members swung and jiggled, all of them beautiful snowflakes, each in their own unique way. Which isn't to say I looked. It was mostly just a question of seeing them out of the corner of my eye. (Okay, I may have peeked at Ben a tiny bit, and let me just point out that his didn't jiggle. It had too much heft.)

You totally know where I'm going with this, don't you? Yup, talk about your half-man/half-beast sightings! But at that point, I'm not sure that best described the Bigfoot hunters, or me, barely able to control myself.

No, not really. The whole situation was undeniably erotic, but I'd spent enough time in locker rooms to know how to deal with situations like this.

Down boy, I said to my own penis, and apart from a bit of sullen twitching, it acquiesced to my command. Then I started to undress myself.

Gunnar, meanwhile, didn't move. He was just as stunned as I was by this turn of events, and was also gaping a little, except not in a sexual way.

"What about the Bigfoot site?" he said at last.

"Oh, we passed that a while ago," Ben said, slipping into the water, the best parts sinking into the murk.

"It'll still be there when we're done," Clive said, following Ben into the pool.

"But..." Gunnar said.

"When in Rome," I said to him, and I buttoned my own pants.

But then I did turn away, from Gunnar at least, because the last thing in the world I wanted to see was my best guy friend naked.

In fairness, we didn't spend the whole day in the hot springs. After an hour or so, we dried ourselves off, then headed back the way we'd come. We had to ford the river to reach the actual spot where Bigfoot had been sighted (and I'd only brought one pair of shoes). But we didn't see anything of the creatures themselves, not even any more partial footprints.

That night, Katie made another great dinner: some of the trout she and Clive had caught grilled with lemon and dill on a skillet over the fire, along with a salad of wild greens Leon had collected that afternoon. And about the time Ben pulled out a home-made blueberry pie, it occurred to me that maybe finding Bigfoot just wasn't all that important to this gathering of Bigfoot hunters—that it was more about the journey, not the destination. It was this weird combination of Unstoppable Career Drive and Passionate Aimlessness. Maybe it was like me and Kevin, when I hadn't wanted to call him, because once I did that, I knew I might have to deal with the fact that he didn't want to get together with me. Maybe it was better that Bigfoot be left a mystery too—and on some level, everyone here knew it.

The next morning as Gunnar and I were rolling up our tent, he said to me, "Ben says he's planning a trip to Eastern Washington next week. Someone found a cave in the Selkirk Mountains that could be a Sasquatch lair."

"Ah," I said. "Great."

"What?"

"Oh, come on, Gunnar. These 'expeditions'?"

"What about 'em?" His face was completely blank, innocent almost.

I lowered my voice and leaned in closer. "I'm just not sure these guys are all that hot to find Bigfoot."

Gunnar leaned away from me, even as I was leaning in, like I had some kind of contagious disease, or maybe just bad breath.

"You're crazy," he said. "Of course they are." He started cramming a down sleeping bag into its stuff sack. "Why would everyone be here if they didn't want to find Bigfoot?"

I immediately thought of a ton of reasons: for Katie, it was a chance to show off her new campfire recipes. For Ben, it was a chance to relive a moment of childhood magic. And for Clive and Leon, it was a chance to have a purpose, to be someone authoritative and special. Meanwhile, they all got a chance to sit in hot springs in the forest and eat ice cream cake before dinner.

But Gunnar really *did* want to find Bigfoot. He didn't want to hear what I was saying. So I carefully tried to put the paper lantern back on the light bulb.

"Yeah, you're probably right," I said.

"You think we're not serious," he muttered, even as he kept stuffing that sleeping bag. "You think this whole thing is stupid."

Wait a minute, I thought. Ben and the others were the ones who had led Gunnar on, with all their talk of partial footprints and Bigfoot blimps. But now he was mad at *me*?

"No," I said. "I just meant—"

"Well, it's not! You hear me? It's *not*!"

He finished stuffing the bag. It was packed in so tight there was even room left over.

"Gunnar..."

"*What*?"

He stared at me, a look in his eyes that I'd never seen before, not on his face, not on anyone's. If I'd run into him some early morning on my way to an outhouse in Stehekin, I might even think he wasn't human.

This wasn't like Gunnar.

"Nothing," I said. "Are you okay?"

"I'm fine. I'm just *fine*."

I looked over at Katie, standing nearby, watching us warily. Which I realized was kind of ironic. I'd started this venture thinking that we had the other crazy Bigfoot searchers to worry about, and now here they were worried about us.

By the time we'd packed the car, Gunnar had calmed down again. We said our goodbyes to Ben and the others, and Gunnar and I had a pleasant enough drive home. But I was still kind of freaked out. This wasn't like Gunnar's other obsessions, all the things he'd done in the past. Something about this one was different, but for the life of me, I couldn't figure out what.

CHAPTER SEVEN

The following Saturday night, Vernie invited me to a dinner party at her house. I hadn't been to that many actual dinner parties in my life, except sort of lurking in the background when my parents had them, but I knew enough to wear a button-down shirt and nice shoes. (But a tie? No, no tie, I decided.)

I admit I was nervous. I didn't know Vernie's friends. What if I said the wrong thing? What if I used the wrong fork? (Although, honestly, has anyone in the history of the universe ever truly cared if you use the wrong fork? And if anyone did, why would *you* care? It would just mean they were a total dick.)

Mostly, though, I really liked Vernie, and I didn't want her knowing yet what a pathetic dud I was.

I rang the doorbell, and a tall thin man with white hair and long white goatee answered the door. He looked like a cross between Uncle Sam and a scarecrow.

"Hi," I said. "I'm Russel?"

"Well, come on in, Russel," he said, so I did. "I'm Elliott." And we shook hands.

Something smelled really good, but by that point, I already knew that Vernie could cook.

"Russel!" Vernie said, coming in from the kitchen. "You're here."

"I am," I said stupidly. I handed her a bottle of wine I'd brought—I knew enough about dinner parties to at least do that. But getting that whiff of how good dinner smelled and seeing her sleek blue dress and the silver combs in her hair, I was suddenly wishing I'd spent more than nine bucks.

"These are my friends," Vernie said. She nodded to the scarecrow-meets-uncle Sam. "Elliott Gutzman." I held out my hand to shake his again, and then I realized that we'd already "met" once, and I'd already shaken his hand. To his credit, he just smiled and shook it again.

"And this is Misty Meyers." She was short and sort of squat with wiry grey hair.

"Hi," I said, shaking her hand too. What was the deal with me suddenly spending all this time around old people? A coincidence, I guess.

Vernie stepped up next to me and put her hands on my shoulders, like she was presenting me on *American Idol*. "Russel saved my life," she said, then went on to explain what had happened that day at the lake.

Elliott and Misty oohed and aahed, and since it was something real I had done, not a finger-painting posted on the refrigerator, I was actually sort of proud.

Then someone else stepped into the room from the hallway—he must have been using the bathroom.

He definitely wasn't old. He was only a little older than I was, maybe twenty-five or twenty-six.

And he was so hot I almost needed my sunblock. He had dark hair and skin—he was Indian American—with a small, lean body and a cotton jacket (unlike me, he'd worn a tie). But he wasn't cocky-hot. It was more of an approachable cuteness, like Manish Dayal, except with more hair gel. I mean, he had dimples.

"Oh!" Vernie said. "Russel? This is my friend Felicks." Vernie was noticeably more excited than when she'd introduced me to Elliott or Misty.

Felicks looked at me and smiled, and I smiled back.

"Russel?" Vernie went on. "Felicks spells his name F-E-L-I-C-K-S. And Felicks? Russel spells his name with one 'l'."

Oh, my God, I thought. *Vernie is trying to set me up!* What, did she think that every guy who spelled his name in an unusual way was also gay? Well, okay, she was right about that, but still.

The room had suddenly gotten very quiet, with Misty and Elliott looking at me and Felicks, then smirking at each other. They had to know this was a set-up too. For one thing, we were the only two guests under the age of sixty.

But honestly? I didn't really care. And my nervousness? It was suddenly (mostly) gone. That seems counter-intuitive, I know. Who doesn't get nervous when they're set up with someone else—especially when that someone is as adorable as Felicks? But there was something demystifying about it too. Now I knew what this dinner party was really all about, and maybe how to act. And truthfully? I couldn't remember the last time anyone had made such a big fuss over me about anything. And while I wasn't even close to being in Felicks' league looks-wise, it was flattering to think that Vernie thought I was.

"Now, Russel," Vernie said with a knowing little smile, "what's your drink?"

I joined in on her smile. "Whiskey sour."

She moved toward the bar. "Felicks?"

"Do you know how to make a Negroni?"

Vernie rolled her eyes. "Do I know how to make a Negroni?" And she turned and busied herself with the cocktails.

Felicks stepped closer to me, smiling, sizing me up. I wasn't as nervous as before, but I still couldn't help thinking: *Great. Not only is he a lot better looking than I am, he also already knows his "drink." And it's one that I've never even heard of.*

"So how do you know Vernie?" we both said at exactly the same time.

Then we laughed awkwardly. So much for my not being nervous.

He sort of bowed to me, and I went first.

"Well..." I said.

"He saved my life!" Vernie called from over by the bar. Clearly, she was listening in. And if there had been any doubt before that this was a set-up—and there hadn't been—there *really* wasn't any now.

Felicks' eyes never left me. "Is that true?" he said.

I nodded, and then I (modestly) told the whole story again.

Felicks listened and nodded back, either duly impressed or faking it well enough that I bought it.

Meanwhile, Elliott and Misty faded back into a conversation of their own.

When I was done telling the story, I asked Felicks, "So how do you know Vernie?"

"Oh, I was friends with her son," he said. "Back in high school."

"And now he works as a publicist," Vernie said, suddenly appearing and handing us our cocktails. "I ran into him at a screening a couple of months ago, and I saw how well he'd grown up, and I knew I wanted to be his friend."

"You have a son?" I said to Vernie. She'd never mentioned having kids before. But the second I said it, it occurred to me that he might be dead or a drug addict or something—that I might have just stumbled into something awkward.

But then Felicks said, "A daughter too." To Vernie, he said, "She's in Phoenix now, right?"

"That's correct," Vernie said. And before I could ask anything more about her kids, she turned and headed back toward the kitchen. "I need to check on dinner. Don't be shy with the smoked salmon on the coffee table!"

This was odd. Was Vernie estranged from her kids? I glanced around the room, but I didn't see any pictures of people who could plausibly be her children. I couldn't help but wonder what the story was. I would've killed for a mom like her.

I turned back to Felicks and smiled again. I wanted to ask him more about Vernie's kids, but it felt like kind of a betrayal somehow. So instead we talked about how most publicists still didn't really understand social media.

* * *

Dinner was Beef Wellington with roasted vegetables and Yukon finger potatoes.

"My dear, it looks *amazing*," Misty said. And I have to admit, it did. I guess I'd heard of Beef Wellington before, but I couldn't have told you that it was beef wrapped in this elaborate pastry.

"Oh, it's nothing," Vernie said, before setting off on a ten-minute story about how incredibly complicated it had all been to make.

"You're as good a cook as you are a writer," Elliott said.

"Oh, please!" Vernie said. "You're the master screenwriter in this room, and you know it. Elliott was nominated for an Oscar."

"So were *you*," Elliott said.

"You were?" I said to Vernie, surprised. She had kids I didn't know about *and* she'd been nominated for an Oscar? What else wasn't she telling me? Did she have dead bodies chopped up and stored in pickle jars down in the basement?

Vernie shrugged it away. "Oh, please, for a short film. That was nothing. It doesn't count."

"Of course it counts," Elliott said.

"It does *not*." Then, with comic timing perfect enough to rival Melissa McCarthy, she hesitated for just the right amount of time and said, "We'll all watch the DVD after dinner."

Everyone howled.

We kept talking, and I learned that Elliott had been one of three screenwriters on a movie called *The Wonder of It All* that had been nominated for Best

Original Screenplay back in the 1970s. I'd never seen it, but I'd definitely heard of it.

"The first time I met the other two writers was the night of the Oscars. Which tells you a lot about how screenwriting in Hollywood works."

It does? I thought. What did it tell me? I didn't know, but I wanted to.

Elliott dished for a bit about how the leads of *The Wonder of It All* were totally fucking each other in real life, and how the actor deliberately pretended to dump the actress the night before they filmed this big, dramatic break-up scene—and she ended up winning an Oscar as a result, which, after they got back together, made the guy so jealous that he later ended up dumping her again for real.

Then Vernie said, "Oh! But let's not forget that Misty here has actually won a Tony Award."

"Yes, I'm one-quarter of the way to my EGOT," said the seventy-ish Misty, wryly, and everyone at the table laughed again. (EGOT is an acronym that stands for people who have won all four of the major entertainment awards—the Emmy, the Grammy, the Oscar, and the Tony. If there had been any doubt whether Felicks was gay—and there really, really wasn't!—there wouldn't have been when I saw him laugh at Misty's joke. Okay, yes, I suppose there are plenty of gay people who don't know what "EGOT" stands for, people like Boston, but I'll just say it: I probably wouldn't be interested in dating them.)

Then Misty told a story about a play she once wrote about Noah's ark, and she had it in her head that she wanted to use real animals on stage. At first, there was a sheep, a goat, and a llama, but the animals kept crapping and peeing, and it was a serious play, and everyone was convinced it would distract the audience. So she rewrote the play so it was a peacock, a ferret, and a dog, but they had exactly the same problem with the peacock and even the dog, who would get nervous and pee in front of the preview audiences. So finally, they cut the live animals completely.

"Then opening night came..." Misty said. "And the backstage toilet flooded."

We all cracked up.

"I kid you not! It really did. And that was just the start of it. The following morning, the critics all took another crap all over that play. One of them actually said, 'It would have been perfect if they'd dared to use live animals.' I should've known it was doomed from the start."

When we were finally done laughing, I said, "Your lives sound like they were so exciting."

"We're not dead yet!" Vernie said, and everyone laughed again.

I couldn't help but blush. "I just meant that your lives seem a little like movies themselves. So cinematic."

"Everyone's life is cinematic," Vernie said, taking a well-timed swig of wine. "You just need to know when to fade to black."

I looked at Felicks and smiled. He grinned back, dimples and all. That was a pretty great line, and we both knew it.

* * *

Dessert was chocolate fondue (deliberately kitschy). Vernie asked for my help carrying it all in from the kitchen.

"What do you think of him?" she asked me as she stirred the chocolate, barely bothering to whisper.

"He's great," I said, trying hard not to roll my eyes.

"Isn't he *adorable*? Just so you know, I considered asking him out for a little tea and sympathy myself." This was a reference to a famous play from the 1950s, *Tea & Sympathy*, where an older woman seduces a younger, possibly-gay guy, and I appreciated that Vernie didn't feel like she needed to explain the joke.

Her eyes found me again. "You're not mad, are you? That I set you up?"

"No. I'm actually sort of flattered." It was the truth.

"Grab the plates, would you? And the fruit?" This was a tray of strawberries, sliced pineapple, and orange slices for the fondue.

Together, we carried dessert into the dining room. As Vernie was passing out the metal skewers, I cleared a place for the fruit. But before I got halfway around the table, Vernie said to me, "Careful."

I looked. Elliott had been holding his skewer out to one side, and I'd almost backed into it.

"Oh, sorry," Elliott said.

"Oh!" Vernie said. "That's it! I just saved your life!"

I looked at her.

"Remember? I dreamt I was going to save your life?" She turned to the rest of the table and told them all about her prophecy.

"Um, that wouldn't exactly have *killed* me," I said.

"Sure, it would've! He almost impaled you. It would been like Vlad the Impaler."

"I don't think that counts."

"It does. It absolutely does!"

I looked at the table. "What do you guys think?"

"I don't think so," Misty said.

"Nope," Elliott said.

Felicks gave Vernie a helpless shrug. "Sorry."

Vernie pretended to be outraged. "I made Beef Wellington for you people. *Beef Wellington!* Fine. But just for that, there will be no after-dinner liqueur!"

After dessert, we retired to the living room where we talked for hours. At the end of every story, I was pretty much thinking, *Nothing even halfway that interesting has ever happened to me.*

But eventually, Felicks stood up and said, "Well, this has been great—really—but I should get going."

"But the party's just getting started!" Vernie said. Then she looked at me and said, "This is a really dangerous neighborhood. Why don't you walk Felicks to his car?"

Queen Anne is, of course, just about the least dangerous neighborhood in all of Seattle. But I'd been about to leave too, so gave my heartfelt goodbyes to Vernie and the others, then followed Felicks outside.

"She's not very subtle, is she?" Felicks said once we'd hit the sidewalk.

I laughed. "No. But that's part of what's so great about her."

"So," he said. "Are we gonna go out or what?"

"I'm not really sure we have a choice." I thought for a second, then I said, "Can I ask you a personal question?"

"I guess so."

"What do you think of PrEP?"

"Huh?"

"You know. HIV drugs for the HIV-negative."

Felicks looked a little surprised. "Why do you wanna know?"

"I had this experience with a guy lately," I said. "A bad experience. And, well, before we go out, I just kind of wanted to know if we were on the same page." Part of me couldn't believe I was asking this outright. I think it had something to do with Vernie, the way she talked. I guess her openness was contagious.

"Ah." Felicks scrunched up his face. "Well, actually, I'm on it. As of about six months ago—my gay doctor's idea. But that doesn't mean I'm a slut, and it sure doesn't mean I'm willing to risk my life on some new drug. I mean, I don't have unsafe sex."

"Yes," I said. "I'd love to go out with you."

"That was the right answer, huh?"

I beamed. "It absolutely was."

CHAPTER EIGHT

So the following Wednesday night (my next evening off), Felicks and I went on a date.

We met at the Pike Place Market pig—this metal sculpture that everyone in Seattle knows about, so people always say, "I'll meet you at the pig!"

We walked around the market for a bit, checking out the stalls of produce and fresh seafood. Houseboats in Seattle aren't really anything like they are in the movies, but the Pike Place Market looks exactly the way it should. There are stalls of perfectly arranged fruit, and fish mongers, and glass cases of fresh pastry and cheese, and endless racks of these fantastic flower bouquets (some for, like, five bucks each). And no movie can capture the smells of the market—the spices, the coffee beans, the roasting skewers of meat, the hint of the ocean.

"So I gotta ask," I said later, after we'd disappeared down into the maze-like shopping area below the market stalls. "What's the deal with Vernie and her kids?"

"Why is there a deal?" Felicks said.

"She's just never mentioned them before. It seems strange."

"How long have you known her?"

Now I was embarrassed. "Um, not long." How many times had I talked to her? Twice? "But I guess we have—I don't know. A kind of a connection? I like her a lot."

"She's your Kathy Griffin?"

"Maybe." I wasn't surprised that Felicks understood, but I was glad he did. "I know it's none of my business. I was just curious."

"Well, Luke and I were friends in high school. I guess he complained about his parents—they were divorced. But it seemed like normal stuff. I don't remember anything specific."

"He hasn't said anything lately?"

"We're not really friends any more. Well, Facebook friends. I could ask him for you."

"No. That seems creepy."

"Why are you curious?"

"Oh, hey, look," I said. "It's Dan Savage." This is a really famous Seattle writer, and he was right across from us, pointing to a glass bong in the window of one of the shops.

Dan writes a really well-known advice column about sex, Savage Love, that's syndicated all over the world. He's sort of a celebrity too, always appearing on *Bill Maher* or CNN to talk gay issues or politics. Oh, and a few years back, he created the It Gets Better Project, telling bullied gay teens that, well, it gets better.

Felicks and I watched him for a moment, trying to be discreet. Dan is tall and thin with salt and pepper hair, older, but boyish. He turned and said something to the guy with him—his husband Terry, I realized. I'd seen Terry in photographs before—he'd co-founded It Gets Better with Dan—but I hadn't even noticed he was there. I couldn't help wondering what it would be like being married to someone famous like Dan Savage, someone who has an opinion about everything, and someone everyone has an opinion about.

"Shall we get some dinner?" Felicks said.

"We absolutely should," I said.

We ate at this place called the Crab Pot, a restaurant inside one of the downtown waterfront piers. I couldn't help but notice that people were looking at Felicks. But why wouldn't they? Felicks was cute. Or maybe they were looking at both of us—I mean, I'm not exactly pigeon guts. We were two cute boys out on a date.

The Crab Pot is a total "gimmick" business, but unlike Bake, it's actually a pretty good gimmick. First, they come and spread butcher paper all over your table. Then they bring a big bucket of steamed clams and mussels and shrimp and crab and corn on the cob and red potatoes, and they dump it right onto the butcher paper. They wrap you up in a plastic bib, and then you eat it all with your hands, breaking the crab open with little hammers and nutcrackers, and dipping it all in seafood sauce or butter.

"What can I get you to drink?" the waiter asked after we'd sat down and before they'd dumped the seafood.

"Whiskey sour," I said, feeling a little self-conscious about it.

Felicks ordered a black Russian. That wasn't what he'd had at Vernie's, and I wondered what *that* said about him. He'd already changed his drink?

"Can I also get a glass of ice water?" I said to the waiter. "And some olive oil for the bread? Oh, and I dropped my napkin."

After the waiter left, Felicks leaned in and sort of smirked, saying, "Aren't we a bossy bottom?"

"Um, I'm not sure I'd make any assumptions about that."

"Ohhh. That's *very* interesting."

Apparently, we'd skipped the flirting and gone straight to talking about sexual positions. And incredibly, I wasn't blushing.

"So what do you think of Dan Savage?" I said. It was funny that we'd just seen him, because asking another gay guy about Dan Savage is basically the "gay date" equivalent of one straight person asking another if they wanted to have kids. Almost every gay person has an opinion about Dan Savage, and that opinion usually tells you a lot about how compatible you are.

"Well," Felicks said. "I mean, there's It Gets Better."

I nodded. Every gay guy starts out talking about Dan Savage by acknowledging that It Gets Better was a really big, important deal.

"Everyone says he's bi-phobic," Felicks went on, "but I don't really see that, at least not anymore. I mean, yeah, he's opinionated, but that's his whole shtick. He's hard on everyone. Although I hate it when people say, 'I offend everyone—that must mean

I'm doing something right!' Yeah, or maybe you're just an asshole."

I laughed out loud. That is *exactly* what I thought about comics and pundits who said that about offending everyone—and for whatever reason, it's almost always the assholes who say it.

"I loved what he said to the bisexuals who say, 'I fall in love with *people*, not their genitals.' He was like, 'Dude, I don't fall in love with genitals either. I just happen to be gay, get over it. Bisexuality is a sexual orientation, not a fucking higher calling.'"

I sort of guffawed. I hadn't heard that particular Dan Savage quote, but it sounded exactly like him.

"I'm getting sort of tired of Dan's big idea about how everyone should be more open to open relationships," Felicks said. "What does he call it? Being 'monogamish'? I agree with him about how honesty is important, and that whatever couples decide between themselves is fine with me. But Dan is always, like, people aren't meant to be monogamous, people need variety. And there's sometimes this sense that he thinks that people who *are* monogamous are somehow repressed or immature, you know? And that's fine, I see his point, but it's such a 'male' point of view. Not even a 'gay male' point of view, but a male one. I mean, if straight guys could be in more open relationships, if more women were interested in non-monogamy, I totally think they'd go for it. But most women aren't. Before feminism, husbands got to sleep around because it was just 'part of their nature'. After feminism, husbands still get to sleep around, only for slightly different reasons. What about what women actually want? Then again, Dan is saying something that no one's ever really said before—the whole idea that couples can decide for themselves how they want to live their lives. And obviously there's going to be a big push-back for an idea like that, so maybe Dan's just preemptively defensive or something. I mean, he's a lot more tolerant and understanding of the people who disagree with him than the people who disagree with him are to him. You know?"

See what I mean about the Dan Savage question being a really interesting one, especially on a first date between two guys? And for the record, I mostly agreed with everything he'd said.

At that point, the waiter brought our drinks (and my ice water, and a new napkin, but he forgot the olive oil).

After the waiter left, I said to Felicks, "What do *you* think about monogamy?"

Felicks opened and closed his nutcracker. "Well, what do *you* think?"

"Huh?"

"I've already talked too much. You talk too much now."

What's this? I thought. *A guy who's aware when he's talked a long time?* I had thought the "Y" chromosome made that impossible.

"I want monogamy," I said. "It's not like I think not being monogamous is a sin or anything. I agree with Dan that it's all about what you decide for yourself, that it's a question of openness and honesty. And I think it's stupid, the whole idea about how an open relationship could never work, that people would get jealous and all that. Well, sure, maybe some people. And I'm sure it's hard sometimes for every-one. But monogamy can be hard too, right? It's not like monogamous people never have problems. I hate how so many people can only see the world from *their* point of view—that they don't ever try to see it any other way." I paused, and Felicks nodded.

"But yeah," I went on, "the guy I end up with, I want us to be monogamous. It's partly safety. I don't want diseases—none of the existing ones, none of the new ones that might pop up. And it's not a paranoid-jealousy thing. I just like the idea of sex being something special, something you share with the person you love. Maybe that'll change when I get older. But for the time being, that's what I want."

"A romantic, huh?"

"Yeah, I guess."

Felicks smiled. "Me too."

Dinner was fantastic.

First, it was just plain good. I love seafood, and there's nothing quite as great as freshly steamed clams and mussels and shrimp and crab.

But it was also fun to be eating with your fingers from this heaping mound of food right in front of you. For the first time in my life, I wondered if this was what people felt like when they came into Bake—that it was worth the extra cost because it was "fun."

But this was more than that. Eating shellfish on a date with a hot guy can be dangerously erotic, especially for a couple who had skipped the flirting stage and gone right to talking about sexual positions.

You have to peel the shrimp, gently pulling back the skin, revealing the tender meat inside. The crab legs are hard and slick, and when you crack them open, the brine sometimes squirts up into your eyes. And some of the mussels aren't open all the way, so you have to slip your finger into the shell, feeling the silky softness inside.

There was lots of dripping and slurping and licking, and everything got sticky fast. And all the while, I was looking at Felicks, staring into his brown eyes, watching his mouth, watching his tongue, and being pretty thankful that the plastic tablecloth hung down far enough that the waiter and the other diners couldn't see the front of my pants.

Afterward, we went for a walk along the waterfront. We both knew exactly where this date was heading— you can only slurp down the insides of so many mollusks with a date as cute as Felicks before these things simply become destiny.

But I could already tell that a big part of the fun of this night was in the anticipation. Besides, we'd just eaten. So we decided to ride this giant Ferris wheel called the Seattle Great Wheel, which is located on one of the piers. It was night now, so it was lit up in neon colors, all flashing in the dark, rising up over the black, sloshing abyss of Elliott Bay.

Each glass car seats four people, two on each side. The pier was crowded, and there was a line behind us, but as we were boarding, I asked the attendant, "Do you think we could get a car to ourselves?" And she smirked and nodded. I guess it was also clear to everyone else exactly where this date was headed.

Once the door was closed, the glass car started to rise into the night sky. We were facing into the city, looking into the lights of the downtown skyscrapers, and we were surrounded by the neon in the lattice of the wheel itself—green and purple and blue and yellow. It was like rising backward into a dream, except for the fact that the roof of the pier down below us was completely covered with pigeon poop.

Felicks and I sat side by side, staring out at the colors. When our car reached the other side of the wheel, we switched seats so we could stare out at the water. A ferry was leaving for the other side of the sound, a little island of light cutting across a literal sea of darkness.

"We never talked about your job," I said. "All through dinner."

"Yours either," he said.

"Yeah, but that was sort of by design. I mean, what is there to say?"

He smiled. I'd told him about my two jobs when we'd met at Vernie's, how pathetic they are.

"Do you like it?" I said.

"I do."

"And what exactly does a publicist do?"

He thought for a second, staring down at the ferry. Green neon shone on his face even as he slipped me a sly grin. "It's the job of a publicist to convince someone he wants something, even if he didn't necessarily want it before."

"I see," I said, nodding. "What if he *does* want it? What if he wants it bad?"

"Then my job gets a whole lot easier."

I guess technically we were back to flirting. But I'd never flirted so brazenly before in my life. We might as well have been lubing each other up.

Then we were kissing, still on the seat, the green

neon turning to blue then purple. He tasted minty, which made me wonder when he'd had a chance to slip in a breath mint without me looking. Or who knows? Maybe he was so perfect that his mouth always tasted that way.

Things could have gone further, but let's face it: we were in a glass Ferris wheel car, and that just seemed tacky.

When the ride was over, I said, "Where now?"

As if I didn't already know we were heading back to his apartment.

Just so you know, this wasn't something I usually did—sex on a first date. Although you could argue that dinner at Vernie's was a date-of-sorts, so this was technically a "second" date. Even so, I had a firm four-dates-before-any-sex policy with guys.

Okay, maybe it wasn't all that firm. Maybe it was more of a general guideline. But I had sometimes stuck to it before.

I know what you're thinking: how can he have even a vague, sporadically-enforced four-dates-be-fore-sex policy if he's also done random online hook-ups?

Remember what I said about fuck buddies—that the point was just sex and not romance or a relation-ship, and there usually wasn't any overlap between the two? That was true of hook-ups too. Get in and get out, pun partially intended.

But actual "dates" are something very different. That's when you're talking about a guy where you think there might actually be the potential for a relationship, for romance. And I think it's totally true that too-early sex can really ruin that potential. It puts it in a different category—something casual, something unimportant. If nothing else, it lessens that fantastic sense of mystery and suspense in those first few weeks of dating.

I'm sorry if this sounds confusing, but I really don't think it is.

Anyway, my night out with Felicks definitely *was* a date, and I was totally opting to violate my four-dates-before-sex rule. Why?

I had no choice: the bivalves had spoken.

Felicks lived on First Hill, just above downtown. He had a roommate, but he was out at the moment. (I couldn't help but wonder if he was *deliberately* out. I hadn't seen Felicks text anyone, but maybe he'd done it when I hadn't been looking, or maybe they'd planned it all out in advance. I wasn't sure whether to be flattered or insulted by this possibility.)

The apartment was nicer than Boston's—Pier One, maybe, not Ikea. But it wasn't so nice that I felt like Felicks and I were in wildly different categories of success. He didn't seem to be a neat-freak either. I couldn't help but think: *Oh! We're compatible in the cleanliness regard too.*

I noticed a strange smell. It had been so long since I'd smelled it that it took me a second to place it.

Cigarette smoke.

Felicks noticed me noticing the smell. "My roommate smokes."

"Ah," I said, nodding sympathetically.

"Can I get you a drink?" he said.

"Sure," I said. "Whatever you have." This was still a date, after all. It's not like we were going to throw off our clothes and have mad, passionate sex then and there. (*Were* we?)

Felicks brought me Coke in a glass with ice cubes.

"Sorry," he said. "Turns out we don't have any alcohol."

That made me feel better. It meant this whole thing hadn't been planned after all. Plus, it at least confirmed that he wasn't an alcoholic—something good to know about a potential husband. (Yes, yes, I was getting waaaay ahead of myself.)

We sat on the couch sipping our Cokes for a second. Then he said, "Oh, hell, it's me."

"What's you?" I said.

"I'm the smoker."

"Oh."

"I don't know why I lied," Felicks said. "I guess I was nervous. I figured it might turn you off."

"No, it's okay." I wasn't crazy about the fact that he smoked, but at least he'd 'fessed up. And everyone has his vice (mine is Pez). Anyway, now I knew why he'd slipped in a breath mint before we'd taken that ride on the Great Wheel—it had been pretty clear we were going to kiss.

"Do you mind if I have one?" Felicks said. "I'm kinda crazy for it. I'll smoke it out on the porch, okay?"

"Yeah, sure, whatever," I said.

So Felicks went out on the porch to light up, and I followed him. How had I not noticed before how jittery he was? Or maybe he hadn't been jittery until just now.

Out on the porch, I asked Felicks, "Do you like living on First Hill?"

He blew a blue cloud away from me. "Well, it's close to downtown."

"And the library," I said.

"You're a reader, huh?"

I nodded. "It's funny though. There are two things about Seattle that I think are totally overrated. The downtown library and the sculpture park."

"Oh, yeah. With some of those sculptures, I feel like we're being *Punk'd*. I mean, what the hell is that big orange thing? If looking at it is supposed to make me think, all I ever think is, 'Why did they make it so incredibly ugly?'"

"And the big 'and' sign? Really? And I totally feel like a prude saying this, but the one with the naked man reaching out for the naked boy, and they're surrounded by all that water—that's just creepy."

Felicks laughed, and I felt the same connection I'd felt with him earlier. I was starting to relax again.

Felicks finished his cigarette, and we headed back inside.

We took seats on the couch again, but this time I happened to glance at the shelf underneath the coffee table. There were comic books, and old TV remotes, and something else—something confusing. Once again, it took a second for my mind to fully register what it was.

A handgun. It was black and sleek. The handle was all one big rubber grip

But even after I realized what it was, I thought: *That must be a toy. Or maybe a lighter.*

It didn't look like a toy. Not at all.

Felicks has a handgun? I thought. And he'd left it out

in the open? He *really* hadn't expected me to come over to his apartment, had he?

Once again, Felicks noticed me noticing.

"That's my roommate's," he said quickly.

The words hung in the air as if on strings, like pieces of a mobile. I think we both realized at the same time that this was exactly what he'd said before, about the cigarette smoke. And he'd been lying. It was pretty clear he was lying this time too.

"No, really," Felicks said. "He's kind of paranoid." Once again, he'd said it just a touch too quickly.

We fell silent. I clutched my Coke. There was cold condensation on the glass, making it feel slick in my hand. It numbed my fingers too. I worried I'd drop it.

"Seriously," Felicks said. "He was gay-bashed a couple of years ago."

"It's cool," I said. "It's none of my business." I wasn't sure what else to say. It was weird to go over to someone's apartment and find a handgun under the coffee table, right? Maybe not in Arkansas, but in Seattle. I sort of expected him to say, "It's not loaded." But he didn't. Which I guess meant it *was* loaded.

I'm sitting three feet from a loaded gun, I thought. The idea made me perspire.

Desperate to change the subject, I looked over at Felicks' bookshelf. He didn't have very many books—it was mostly games and DVDs. But one of the book titles caught my eye right away. *The Tea Party Goes to Washington* by Rand Paul.

"The Tea Party, huh?" I said. "I hope to hell *that's* your roommate's." Then I laughed, because I was certain it was.

But Felicks didn't laugh. He just meekly sipped his drink.

"What?" I said.

"Uh, that really is mine," he said at last.

"Wait," I said. "Go back. You're a Rand Paul supporter?"

He shrugged, and the ice cubes tinkled in his glass. "Sort of, yeah."

"But you're gay," I said. *And a person of color,* I thought. *And not a total idiot.*

"What does that have to do with anything?" Felicks said. "The two-party system is completely broken."

"Yeah," I muttered. "Thanks to people like Rand Paul whose whole strategy is to blow everything up, and then try to blame all the chaos on Obama."

Once again, we both sat in silence for a second. Now our ice cubes weren't even tinkling. Felicks was really a libertarian? Suddenly the loaded handgun made more sense. In a way, so did the cigarette smoking.

"Well," Felicks said. "This got weird fast."

It *had* gotten weird. I guess political compatibility was yet another reason to stick to the four-dates-before-sex rule.

"It's funny," he said. "At dinner, I was already merging our iTunes accounts."

I smiled. "Yeah, me too. But..." Cigarette smoking and little white lies were one thing. And maybe there really was a good explanation for that handgun under the coffee table. But Felicks being a Tea Partier? Give me a fucking break. Trying to see the world from the point of view of other people didn't necessarily mean *dating* them—not if they stood for just about everything you thought was wrong in the world. Just like with Boston, this relationship was doomed before it even started.

"Yeah," Felicks said, nodding.

I stood up to go.

"'Course that doesn't mean we couldn't still fool around," he said.

I looked back at him, at his smooth brown skin, his shiny black hair, perfectly gelled. I could even smell him over the cigarette smoke, the scent of something musky and mysterious. He was a handgun-wielding libertarian, but Felicks was still a hottie.

I considered for a second. "I guess I could stay a little while longer." Just because the date was officially over, it might not be the end of the world if the evening segued into something more like a hook-up.

Hey, I never said I was a perfect person, okay?

CHAPTER NINE

So it was the Fourth of July, but I didn't feel like I had much to celebrate. In case you've forgotten, I'll recap with bullet-points:

- I'd just gone on a pretty disastrous date with Felicks, one made all the more terrible because it had started out so well.
- I had two jobs I totally hated.
- I had a roommate, Gunnar, who was a lunatic.
- I didn't have Kevin.

And speaking of jobs I hated, of course I had to work at Green Lake all day on the Fourth of July, until seven p.m. When I finally got home around eight, Min and her Min-ions were up on the rooftop deck. Every year, the city puts on a fireworks show over Lake Union, and lots of people gather in their boats in the middle of the lake to watch it. The

134

problem is, there are a lot of boats in Seattle, and Lake Union just isn't that big a lake. So it's like this insane boat traffic jam all day long, with people shouting and boats knocking and music blaring, and it doesn't quite make sense because sailboats usually seem so peaceful.

"There's lots of food in the fridge," Min said. "We barbecued."

I wasn't surprised they hadn't waited on me for dinner, but I was a little surprised that Gunnar was with them. Lately, he'd been pretty wrapped up in his Bigfoot research.

I went down and loaded up a plate for dinner. They'd made roasted vegetables and barbecued polenta, which made sense since Min and the Minions were all vegetarian. (And as much as I'd like to use this occasion as another opportunity to bash Trai and Lena, the food was *amazing.* They had grilled carrots and zucchini and onions and portabella mushrooms. They'd actually made this barbecue sauce for the polenta—with peaches, I think. People who say that vegetarian food is lousy or tasteless have clearly never been to Seattle.)

Then I went back up to the deck again to wait for the fireworks show.

Trai was explaining some idea he had. "Data encryption is usually based on mathematical algorithms," he was saying. "Which means it's reversible, to physical quanta. The code can always be cracked, if you're patient and you work at it long enough. But our idea is totally different. This is a encryption based on quantum properties. It's literally impossible to decode, not unless you figure out a way to violate the laws of physics. We already have a prototype code, and we're meeting with some investors next week. It's just casual, but it could lead to something."

Another start-up? I thought. This figured. I was sure it was going to be a huge success, and if Min was involved, she'd probably end up as rich as Gunnar.

And I'd still be making nine-forty an hour.

"Isolate your intellectual property," Gunnar said. "That's what screwed me up when I set up my first corporation. It's different from the prototype. The prototype might change, but the intellectual property won't, not if you define it right. I can walk you through it if you want."

Now, see, this is exactly the kind of thing that I wouldn't have expected Gunnar to know. Sometimes I forget that his head isn't always in the clouds. He gets obsessed about some pretty crazy things, but he can also be surprisingly practical. In truth, his striking it rich with the *Singing Dog* iPhone app was really no fluke. If that hadn't worked out, he probably would have struck gold some other way. And when his current money runs out, he'll just stumble upon some new fortune. It pays to be intellectually curious— literally.

"What about you?" Trai said. "What do you think?"

"Huh?" I said. Trai was speaking to me?

"Of our business idea."

I stared at him stupidly. I didn't know a single thing about physics *or* business (thus the jobs at Green Lake and Bake). But I wasn't about to let Trai know this.

"It sounds great," I said. And then, in a fiendishly clever attempt to change the topic, I said, "Who made the barbecue sauce for the polenta? Peaches, right? It's fantastic."

Trai smiled. "Yeah. Peaches. Lena's recipe." We all looked over at her, talking with Min off to one side.

And then no one said anything. Trai and Gunnar looked back at me like they expected me to say something else.

So much for my brilliant plan to change the topic.

"I had a business idea once," I said. "I may still put it into practice one day."

"Yeah?" Trai said.

"Yeah. Clean airport bathrooms."

"Airports already have bathrooms," Gunnar said.

"Yeah, but they're totally disgusting, because so many people use them. And let's face it, when you're in an airport, sometimes it's late at night or early in the morning, and you have to, you know, *really use the bathroom.* Who wants to do that in an airport bathroom when there's no real privacy? So I figure you could set up a storefront in airports where everyone has their own individual unisex bathroom, and each one is cleaned after each use. It would cost fifteen bucks or something, and you could, like, sell toiletries too—toothbrushes and razors, and maybe have shower stalls. You could just call it Clean Bathrooms. Or maybe something trendy, like Wash or Pipe."

When I finished talking, Trai just stared at me. It wasn't so quiet you could hear a pin drop, because it was Lake Union on the Fourth of July, and there were firecrackers and skyrockets and music blaring from the boats in front of us and the houseboats around us. But Trai was trying to embarrass me. Wasn't he? Maybe it was all in my mind. Maybe it wasn't the greatest business idea in the world, but it wasn't terrible either. Was it?

Finally, Gunnar said, "I love it! I bet you're gonna make a lot of money."

Meanwhile, Trai sort of turned and drifted over toward Min and Lena, and the three of them started murmuring about something. I wanted to tell Trai to go jump in a lake. As chance would have it, there was one very handy!

I ignored him, turning back to Gunnar.

"So what'd you do all day?" I said.

"Huh?" He looked at me. "Oh, you know. The usual."

I actually *didn't* know. What was a "usual" day for Gunnar, since he didn't have to work anymore and was pretty damn weird to begin with? I still had no idea. Maybe one day I could strap a tiny camera on him and see what he ended up doing, like how they do with cats. The results would probably be really surprising, just like how they always are with cats.

I thought about making this joke with Gunnar, but then I saw the distracted expression on his face, so I decided not to.

"You doing anything interesting this weekend?" I asked. The Fourth of July was on a Friday night this year.

He sort of shrugged. Then he looked down at the railing around the top of the boat. Something about it was suddenly fascinating to him.

"Any new Bigfoot sightings?" I said. I kind of hated to go there, since I still felt a little weirdness from that expedition a few weeks earlier. On the other hand, we had to talk about something.

And sure enough, Gunnar immediately perked up again.

"There was a sighting this week over in Icicle Canyon. But it was Class B, so no one's taking it very seriously."

"Class B?"

"There are three kinds of Bigfoot sightings—Class A, Class B, and Class C. Class C are the worst—second-hand reports and legends and things like that. Class B are a little better, because they're first-hand accounts. But they're not clear—they're sightings from a distance or in low light. Class A are the ones that really matter. They're the ones that are close-up, where you can absolutely rule out it being a different kind of animal. The one we were investigating a couple of weeks ago was Class A. And remember Ben's encounter with the Bigfoot up at Stehekin? That was Class A too."

"Is this like close encounters of the third kind?" I asked. I thought for a second. "Wait. Are there three different kinds of close encounters? I mean, of UFOs? Hold on. A close encounter of the third kind is the best kind, right? Like in the movie? So is it the opposite of Class A, B, and C?"

Gunnar shook his head—showing a little too much annoyance, I thought. "No, that's totally different."

"How?" I said, not knowing how else to keep this conversation going.

"There are actually five kinds of close encounters with aliens. A close encounter of the first kind is a UFO sighting, close-up. A close encounter of the second kind is feeling physical effects, like heat or shaking. A close encounter of the third kind is seeing the actual alien. The fourth kind is being abducted, and the fifth kind is actual communication. None of this is about how good or clear the encounter is. With that system, either you have an encounter with aliens or you don't. And if you don't, then it's not a 'close' encounter at all. Get it?"

I nodded, even as I thought to myself, defensively, *Well, it's still* kind *of like Class A, Class B, and Class C.* I mean, I wasn't *totally* wrong, even if I'd forgotten there were also close encounters of the fourth and fifth kind.

Then I realized I was debating observational rating systems for aliens and Bigfoot, and decided maybe it was time to change the topic again.

"No, really," I said to Gunnar. "This barbecue sauce is amazing, and it's made with actual peaches."

Later, after I'd managed to finally pull Min aside from her friends, I said to her, "I'm still worried about Gunnar."

She nodded in the dark. "Yeah, me too."

But right then, the fireworks started.

There are firework shows, and then there are fireworks shows that you see from the roof-top deck of a houseboat on Lake Union. It was like being in the middle of an electric jellyfish.

And then, in the midst of all that sparkling beauty, I happened to glance across the deck and see Trai holding Min's hand.

Min and Trai are dating? I thought.

I did a double-take, but by that time, Min was

already pulling her hand away. She looked my way and smiled. She thought she'd gotten away with the subterfuge—she hadn't seen that I'd seen.

I smiled back, but inside I was groaning. Trai? This figured. Out of all the people in the world—literally, male or female, since Min is bisexual—she had to pick *Trai*? It was even worse that they were friends, that they already knew each other in some sense. That meant it was less likely to be some stupid temporary fling—that there was still a chance she could find out he was a handgun-wielding, Rand Paul-supporting idiot.

The fireworks ended shortly after that. Trai and Lena had to go home, so they said their goodbyes (to Min, without even *offering* to help clean up the kitchen).

As Gunnar, Min, and I tidied up, I couldn't help but wonder why she didn't want me to know about her and Trai. Because she suspected I didn't like him? I knew I should say something, tell her I thought it was okay, but I couldn't find the right words.

Before I knew it, the houseboat was mostly clean, and I was taking a bag of trash out to the dumpster. That meant walking all the way down the dock to the parking lot. In the streets in front of me, and even up on the freeway on the hill, I could hear the huffing of cars—all the people who'd come to Lake Union to watch the fireworks but were now stuck in traffic jams.

I made it to the dumpster and tossed the trash. When I turned around, I saw two figures standing by a car on the other side of the parking lot. It was Trai and Lena.

Kissing.

I couldn't help but stare. They were right under a streetlight, and I was in the shadows, so I didn't think they could see me even if they looked.

But they weren't looking. They were too busy going at it.

Trai is cheating on Min, I thought. This was even better than him turning out to be a handgun-wielding, Rand Paul-supporting idiot. There was no way Min would stay together with him now.

I tried to contain my glee. I was no fan of Trai's, but Min was still one of my two best friends, and I didn't want to see her hurt.

"Hey, Min," I said, back inside the boat. "Can we talk for a sec?" I'd come to her bedroom, but I stood in the doorway. Her bedroom is bigger than mine, but it still doesn't really have room for two people except in bed. On the back wall, she had a poster of Xena Warrior Princess and her sidekick, Gabrielle.

Min looked up from her iPad. "Sure," she said. "Oh, yeah, you wanted to talk about Gunnar. Do you think we should talk to him? Maybe do a Bigfoot intervention?"

"This isn't about Gunnar."

"What's it about?"

I hemmed and hawed.

"Just say it," she said.

"I just saw Trai and Lena kissing. Out in the parking lot."

Min pondered this, but didn't seem shocked.

"You guys are dating, right? I saw you holding his hand up on the deck."

"Oh," she said. "Yeah."

"Well, I hate to drop this on you like this." Sadly, I didn't actually hate it all, but I was determined not to feel any actual joy about it. "I just figured it was something you should know."

Min didn't say anything. Outside the boat, the water sloshed. The waves seemed particularly rough tonight, probably from all the boats trying to get home.

"Are you going to break up with him?" I said. As soon as I said it, I regretted it. It sounded way too eager. Besides, it was none of my business anyway.

"I don't know."

I kept staring.

"It's complicated," Min said.

"Complicated? He's cheating on you. Trust me, this was no peck on the cheek."

Min twisted on her bed. "I'll definitely talk to him."

"Min?" I said.

The lamp on her nightstand flickered. Were we going to lose power? Min looked over at the bulb.

"What's going on?" I asked.

"Why do you think something's going on?" She still wasn't looking at me.

"Well, for one thing, you never told me you were seeing Trai in the first place."

"Yeah, sorry," Min said. "I just knew you don't like him."

"And now you don't seem very upset by what I just told you."

"I *am* upset. I'll talk to him. Thanks. I really appreciate your telling me."

I didn't leave the doorway, just kept looking at her.

"Do you and Trai have an open relationship?" I

asked. This is what Dan Savage was always going on about—what Felicks and I had talked about at dinner.

"No," Min said tightly.

"So why aren't you mad?" Where was the shrieking and the throwing of vases—or at least the Min-equivalent? A confident dismissal followed by a thorough un-friending?

"I am," Min said. "I'm really upset. I am."

I'd seen Min upset before, and this wasn't it.

Okay, I thought, *now I have something else to add to my bullet-point list of things not to celebrate this Fourth of July:*

• Not just one, but two lunatic roommates.

As I was getting ready for bed that night, I got a text from Kevin.

Hey there, wanna come to dinner at Colin's and my place?

I stared at the text on my phone for about ten minutes.

My perfect ex who I wanted to get back together with but who didn't want me anymore was inviting me over to his place for dinner with his probably-just-as-perfect new boyfriend? Once again, this had disaster written all over it.

But if Min could be so completely blasé about Trai seeing Lena, I guess I could do the same with Kevin. So I sent a text back to him saying, Yeah, I'd love to come.

CHAPTER TEN

So I'd been invited to dinner at the apartment of my ex-boyfriend and his new boyfriend. I know I'm making my life sound like all I ever do is go to dinners and parties, which is just so not true. Most of my life is actually spent watching little kids pee in Green Lake, or refilling the quinoa bin at Bake—no lie. But nothing interesting ever happens at those places (except the things I've already told you). For better or for worse, dinners and parties are usually where the action is.

This particular dinner with Kevin and Colin? Beforehand, it seemed both wonderfully civilized and absolutely terrifying. What if I burst into tears in the middle of the soup course? What if they casually brought up the idea of a three-way during the entree? What if Colin challenged me to a duel during dessert?

Basically, I had absolutely no idea what to expect. I just had the unsettling feeling that, as usual, *something* was going to happen.

It took place the very next night, Saturday. From Gunnar's houseboat, I took the SLUT over to Belltown, which is the part of Seattle where Kevin and Colin live. (SLUT stands for South Lake Union Trolley which—true story—is what the city referred to it as right after the train opened. Naturally, once they realized what acronym they were accidentally spelling out, they immediately renamed it the South Lake Union Streetcar. But the first name stuck and now people still mostly refer to it as the SLUT.)

Kevin and Colin lived in a nice new building—so nice that I was sort of scared to see the inside. True, I live in a houseboat on Lake Union, just about the hippest place a person can live in Seattle, but that's only because I happen to have a rich best friend who doesn't mind my freeloading off him, not because of anything I've done. In other words, if I tried to use it to trump their posh Belltown apartment, there was a good chance I'd end up looking ridiculous.

They buzzed me in, and I rode up to the twelfth floor. The elevator smelled like lavender, and I had this annoyed feeling that it was some kind of pretentious new "ambiance" service—like how buildings used to play canned music in their elevators, now they literally pumped different fragrances into them. Hell, maybe they changed it every day—cinnamon one day, lilacs the next.

The door to Kevin and Colin's apartment was already open a little when I reached it, but I knocked anyway.

"Hello?" I said, pushing the door open farther. "It's me." As if they didn't know that, given that they'd buzzed me in only five minutes earlier.

Kevin stepped into the end of the long hallway. "Russel! Come on in." He still had the same impish smile that I remembered so well—so damn mysterious that it would've stumped even Leonardo da Vinci.

"Wow, this is a great place," I said, before I'd even had a chance to register what I was seeing. But then the images of the apartment in front of me finally reached my brain. It was nice, but not so nice that I wanted to slit my wrists. It was sleek and clean, and the furniture was trendy—mostly glass and leather, neither Ikea nor Pier One, but probably from one of the condo specialty shops in Pioneer Square. Still, it was small, almost as small as the front room of Gunnar's houseboat, but it didn't have a good reason to be so compact, so it *felt* more confined. It had a view, but not of anything interesting, like the Space Needle or Elliott Bay. It mostly just looked out on the other nearby apartment buildings.

And geez, that entry hallway sure was long.

Finally, I came to the end where Kevin was waiting. I wasn't sure whether to hug him or not. We'd hugged before, at Uwajimaya, right? But he didn't make a move toward me, didn't open his arms or anything, and I didn't exactly want to throw myself at him, so instead I sort of walked right by him, officially stepping out into the main room.

"It really is a great apartment," I said, totally repeating myself.

"Can I get you something to drink?" Kevin said. "A beer? Wine?"

"Sure," I said.

"Which?"

I was about to ask for a whiskey sour when I realized that hadn't been one of the options. So instead I said, "Maybe a glass of ice water?"

I turned and looked back into the kitchen, which was sort of recessed from the main room.

And that's when I saw Colin. He was cooking dinner. Something sizzled on the stove, and I smelled...curry? Or was it cumin? And what exactly is the damn difference? Colin was slicing avocados.

He was looking right at me, but not smiling. I didn't smile either, just sort of stared at him.

"Russel?" Kevin said, wrestling with the ice machine, getting me my water. "This is Colin. Colin, Russel."

"Hi," Colin said, still not smiling.

But I didn't answer. It was like I *couldn't* answer. I was struck dumb.

You know how some people look better *in* clothes—how the material just sort of hangs off them hinting at the great things underneath, but also covering all their flaws? And you know how some people look better *out of* clothes—how they have some breathtaking attribute, like great arms or a huge dick that they'd be stupid to cover up with material?

Then there are people like Colin where that's a stupid choice, because you just know that he looks as incredible in clothes, with the material falling perfectly off him, as he does out of them, with his great arms and huge dick.

Kevin is hot, and while I was hoping that Colin looked like something that lived under a bridge, I was fully expecting him to be hot too. But I expected him to be ordinary-hot, like Kevin or Felicks. I didn't expect him to be godlike-hot, like Montgomery Clift in his early movies or Matt Bomer now. I'd like to be able to say he was *too* hot—that he was too perfect, that he was plastic, or fake, or generic, or something like that. But I can't say that, because he was just too stunningly handsome.

"I live in a houseboat on Lake Union!" I said.

No one said anything, which made sense, since it was an incredibly stupid thing to say. Colin kept staring at me, not smiling, and Kevin stared at me too, still standing at the refrigerator. For a second, the trickle of water from the ice machine made me think I was peeing my pants.

"But this place is even better," I said, salvaging the moment somewhat (and also heading off any talk of how I was able to afford living in a houseboat on Lake Union). "I mean, I love this location—so close to downtown, but not right in the thick of things."

"Yeah," Kevin said, handing me my water. "We love it. It's close to Colin's school and my work."

"Oh, right," I said. "Amazon."

"Yeah," he said, like he had something to apologize for, which I guess he did since half the city worked there. And also because they're, you know, Amazon.

"Do you like it?" I said. "I don't think I asked you that."

"It pays well, but the hours are crazy."

"What do you do?" Colin asked, mashing the avocados. He was making fresh guacamole.

"Oh," I said, stalling for time, trying to think of some way to make my jobs sound more impressive than they are. "Well, I have two jobs. I work as a lifeguard out at Green Lake. And in this bakery over in U Village."

"Ah." Colin didn't even nod, just squeezed limes into the avocados.

"Where do you go to school?" I asked him.

"Seattle University. Law school."

This told me something important about Colin. I said before that everyone my age in Seattle either has Unstoppable Career Drive or Passionate Aimlessness—well, everyone except me. If Colin was in law school and Kevin was killing himself at Amazon, that meant they both had Unstoppable Career Drive. So it made sense that they were together.

"That must keep you pretty busy," I said.

"Yeah," he said. Then he thought for a second. "Well, not that busy. We go sailing a lot."

"Sailing?"

"Yeah. I have a sailboat. We keep it in a marina on Lake Union. We're out there all the time. Hey, if you live on a houseboat, you've probably seen us."

Remember when I said I wondered who was out sailing on Lake Union on a Thursday night? Well, now I knew. Anyway, I'd been wrong about Colin. He wasn't like everyone else in Seattle in their twenties, with *either* Unstoppable Career Drive *or* Passionate Aimlessness. He was the one guy in the city who had both.

In other words, he was the exact opposite of me.

Dinner was chicken tacos in soft corn tortillas with Mexican rice—and fresh guacamole. As much as I would like to be able to report it was terrible, it actually wasn't.

"How did you guys meet anyway?" I asked them as we ate.

"In school," Kevin said. He'd gone to UC Irvine.

"We were both on the rugby team," Colin said, exchanging a wry little grin with Kevin that I was certain had to do with them regularly soaping each other up in the gym showers.

What the hell *was* rugby anyway? I knew it wasn't that game with the balls and pins. Cricket? And it wasn't polo, the one with the mallets. Suddenly I realized there was this whole game I'd been hearing about all my life, and I had no idea what it was or how to play it. So I had no idea what to say about it.

So I said, "This is really good. Is this curry or cumin in the chicken?"

"Both," Colin said.

"What's the difference anyway?"

"Well, cumin is a spice. Curry is a mix of different spices—including cumin."

"Ah," I said. "Well, it's good."

And then the conversation came to screeching halt. Something smelled like lavender, and then I realized it was me, from the elevator.

"So, Russel," Colin said. "Kevin tells me you're a pretty good baseball player."

I looked at Kevin, who looked a little surprised that Colin had brought that up.

"No," I said. "I mean, I played in high school for about half a semester. But I wasn't ever very good. Not like Kevin."

"Yeah, you were," Kevin said, not really selling it.

"Do you like Amazon?" I asked Kevin.

"Well, it pays well," he said. "But the hours are crazy."

There was a pause when I think we all three realized at the same time that this is exactly what I'd asked Kevin before, and that he'd given me exactly the same answer. On the other hand, it meant that I wasn't necessarily the only one nervous here.

This dinner was rapidly crashing and burning. I think we all realized that at the same time too.

"So tell us, Russel," Colin said. "What do you do for fun?"

"Huh?" I said. "Oh, I don't know. Mostly just hang out."

Colin nodded like I'd actually said something interesting.

"Hey," Kevin said, "remember when Joel Long super-glued all the computer mice to the desks? I thought Valdez was going to have a heart attack."

Stories from high school? I thought. Had we really sunk that low?

But I laughed. "Oh, yeah."

"I wonder whatever happened to Valdez."

"He had a heart attack. He's dead."

"Really? Oh, God, now I feel like an asshole."

"No, sorry, I'm just bullshitting you."

Kevin laughed. "It's all good."

Colin smiled, but that's about it.

"Seriously, Russel," he said. "What's your big thing?"

My "big thing"? I wasn't sure I had one. And what was this business of Colin calling me by my name over and over? Most people didn't do that, not in everyday conversation. Was this some sort of "alpha male" thing—some way he was trying to gain dominance over me? Or maybe I was reading into things again. I was definitely predisposed to not liking Colin.

"Well," I said. "Last week, I went on this search for Bigfoot. We didn't see him, but I guess they did find a partial footprint." I explained a little bit about the expedition. I even mentioned the Bigfoot blimp with thermal-imagining, and the Kickstarter campaign.

"Bigfoot, huh?" Colin said, smirking, totally judging these people he'd never met. "How long have you been into that?"

"Well, it's not really me," I said. "It's my housemate Gunnar. He gets involved with a lot of crazy stuff."

"Good ol' Gunnar," Kevin said, smiling. He knew Gunnar from high school. "How is he?"

"Oh, Gunnar is Gunnar. He's actually rich now." I told them about *Singing Dog*, but I left out the part about that being the reason I was able to live in a houseboat on Lake Union. "That's how he's able to pay for these projects of his, like looking for Bigfoot."

"This Gunnar sounds like a real character," Colin said, and I didn't miss the subtext: *Is there anything interesting about* you?

"What about Min?" Kevin asked.

"Oh, she's working on her PhD, of course."

"Of course!" Kevin said.

"Physics. I guess she and her friends have figured out a way to encrypt information using quantum physics, not mathematic logarithms."

"Algorithms," Colin said.

"What?" I said.

"Encryption uses mathematic *algorithms*. Logarithms are something totally different."

I stared at him for a second. That's when I knew: I wasn't reading into anything when it came to Colin. Unlike with Trai, there was no chance it was all in my mind.

I stared a Colin a second longer, sort of gaping, like I was shocked by what an asshole he was being.

Then I casually turned back to Kevin, ignoring Colin entirely. "Anyway, I keep telling her she needs to devote that great brain of hers to figuring out the secrets of the universe."

"Well, it's only a matter of time."

"Isn't it?"

We ate our tacos. I tried not to make a mess of the tablecloth, but I didn't try that hard.

"So Russel," Colin said, "what are *your* plans?"

It was all I could do not to roll my eyes. "Plans?"

"Well, you're living here in Seattle. In a houseboat on Lake Union. Where do you see yourself in five years?"

I literally froze with my partially-eaten taco halfway to my mouth. Colin was an asshole, but he was a *smart* asshole. He also knew what I knew: that twenty-somethings in Seattle all have Unstoppable Career Drive or Passionate Aimlessness (or, in his case, both). But somehow he'd discovered my shameful secret, that I didn't have *either*. Now he was determined to make sure that Kevin knew it too.

But Kevin came to my defense. He turned to Colin and said, "What is this, a job interview?"

Colin backed off. "I'm just curious."

By this point, I'd just about had it with Colin. He wanted to play the whole "alpha male" game, saying my first name over and over, and flaunting his knowledge of mathematics and Indian spices? Well, I could play that game too. My life wasn't anything to be ashamed of, to get defensive about.

"Well, *Colin*," I said. "I don't know where I'll be in five years. I'm twenty-three years old, so I guess you could say I'm still finding myself. But I did save this lady from drowning earlier this summer, and we've become good friends. And one of the things I *really* like about her is that she doesn't judge people based on things she doesn't understand." Two could play the subtext game.

"Great," Colin said. "Maybe she can help you find Bigfoot."

So basically Colin was challenging me to a duel after all—and he hadn't even waited for dessert.

I didn't need this shit. I pushed my chair back from the table, "You know, I think maybe I should just go."

"No!" Kevin said, but I couldn't help but notice that Colin didn't say a damn thing.

I ran all the way to the SLUT station, but of course I'd just missed the trolley. This late at night, I'd probably have to wait another twenty minutes.

"Russell!" a voice called. "Stop!"

Kevin had followed me. That was kind of fun.

I pretended not to hear him. Why not milk it for a bit?

He reached me at last. "Russel?"

I turned. He was out of breath.

"Look, I'm sorry. Colin's not usually like that."

I just stared at him. I'll admit it: I wanted him to grovel.

"This was my fault," he said. "Inviting you for dinner was a bad idea. I'm really sorry."

I turned away. "It's cool."

"He's jealous, okay?"

Jealous? I thought. That was sort of flattering, a guy like *him* being jealous of me. But what exactly did he have to be jealous about?

"He's heard the way I talk about you," Kevin went on. "That was a really special time in my life. *You* were really special to me."

This was nice to hear too, that Kevin was telling the truth when he'd said he still felt about our high school years the way I felt about them. Unfortunately, it was impossible to ignore that "were" when he was talking about his feelings for me.

"You're *still* special," he said.

Warmer, I thought. *Warmer.*

"Which is why it's probably better if we don't see each other for a while."

Cold, I thought. *Freezing! Sub-Arctic temperatures!*

"I mean, you and I, we've both moved on," Kevin said. "And I really want to be your friend. I *am* your friend—I'll always be your friend. But it's obviously hard for Colin, with your and my past and everything. And I understand that—it would be hard for me if he had a friend like you. I thought enough time had gone by, but maybe it hasn't, not yet. And Colin is my partner now, and I need him to trust me. So how about we be friends—really, really good friends—but friends that just don't see each other for a while?"

This was why Kevin had come running after me? To tell me that he didn't want to see me again, not for "a while"? This scene wasn't ending the way it was supposed to, not at all. But even as I worked through all this, I thought, *This is so Kevin. He's just that great, just that loving.* Problem was, the greatness and love that Kevin was now directing at Colin used to be directed at me.

What could I do? I wanted to take him in my arms and kiss him and say, "Fuck Colin! Let's be together forever, just you and I. You're the perfect guy, and we're perfect together!"

But we weren't perfect together, and Kevin wasn't the perfect guy either. The perfect guy wouldn't be choosing Colin over me.

"Yeah," I said, forcing my head to nod. "You're absolutely right. We shouldn't see each other for a while." *Not until you either dump Colin*, I thought, *or I have such an incredible new boyfriend that he'll even make me forget about you.*

CHAPTER ELEVEN

That night after I got home, I was too annoyed and depressed to sleep. Weirdly, I was the only one in the houseboat. No one had texted me or left a note or anything. But I didn't care. It was sort of nice to have some privacy for a change. I climbed up onto the roof-top deck and stared at the Seattle skyline. I'm sure it was just as amazing as always—it was a beautiful night in July—but I barely noticed. I couldn't stop thinking about dinner and what Kevin had said to me afterward.

It was after ten, but there were still a couple of boats out on the water. Could one of them be Kevin and Colin, out for a late-night sail? The other thing I was thinking was: *How come I never have a bazooka when I need one?*

I was just about to fire up one of my hook-up apps—er, "dating" apps—when I heard creaks on the steps behind me.

"Russel?"

I turned. Min.

"Hey, there." I looked around for the Min-ions, but I didn't see them. "You alone?"

"Yeah. Where's Gunnar?"

I shrugged.

She took a seat next to me, and we stared out at nothing together.

"How was your dinner?" Min said.

"Terrible," I said.

I told her what happened.

"Oh, my God, what a *dick*," Needless to say, she was talking about Colin.

"I know, right?"

"He's jealous of you. You know that, right? The only reason a person would act like that is if he's jealous."

"That's what Kevin said. Right before he told me he never wanted to see me again."

"So maybe Colin has a *reason* to be jealous."

I looked at her.

"It's a thought," she said. "Maybe Kevin's said something to him about his feelings for you. Or maybe Colin just senses it. So maybe that's why Kevin doesn't want to see you—because he's afraid of acting on his feelings."

This was so obvious I didn't know why I hadn't thought of it myself. Was it still so hard to imagine, the idea that someone could actually be in love with me?

"It doesn't matter anyway though," I said. "He said he doesn't want to see me."

Min didn't say anything, just sort of nodded.

"Russel, can I talk to you for a second?"

"Sure," I said. There was something in her voice, like she had something important to tell me. I know

I'd fallen for this before, when I'd assumed Gunnar had something important to tell me and it turned out to be that he'd embarked on a search for Bigfoot. But Min was different—more straightforward, at least with stuff like this.

I didn't just look at her. I turned my chair toward her. I gave her my full attention.

But she didn't say anything. She looked out at the water.

Finally, she said, "This is hard."

"What," I joked, "are you coming out to me as straight?"

Min didn't laugh. Hell, she didn't even smile.

"Wait," I said. "*Are* you straight? It's totally cool if you are."

"No, that's not it."

"Well, what is it? Come on, Min. It's me. There isn't anything you can't tell me."

As soon as I said this, I thought: *Is that true? Is there anything Min could tell me that would make me not like her?* Maybe if she confessed to being a murderer or something, although if her victim was Trai, we might still be good.

"It's about Trai and Lena."

Speak of the devil, I thought.

"Aw, Min, I'm sorry."

"About what?"

"Well, aren't you telling me that Trai left you for Lena?"

"No, no, Trai and I are still together."

"And you've worked it all out with Lena?"

"Sort of. It's complicated."

"I bet. I can only imagine how hard it must be to be around her."

Min sort of half held up a hand. "Russel, you don't understand. That's what I'm trying to tell you. There's something you don't know about Trai and Lena and me. Some important."

I admit that now I was intrigued. What didn't I know about Trai and Lena?

"We're together," Min said.

"You and Trai?"

"No. Both of them."

"Ohhhh," I said. "Wait. Go Back. What? Do they both know about the other?"

"No, Russel, you still don't understand. We're all dating each other. The three of us. Together. I think I might be polyamorous."

Polyamorous? If you lived in Seattle, you sort of had to be in a cave not to have heard this word. I knew it had something to do with multiple partners. Like a group marriage, I guess. But in my entire life, I'd hardly given it a passing thought, except feeling a mild annoyance when all the Seattle polyamorists tried to claim it was exactly like being gay—and that gay people were hypocrites for not totally wrapping themselves around their movement. You could even say it was a small pet peeve of mine: gay people spend decades killing themselves, fighting like hell for public acceptance, bravely coming out in the face of rejection and discrimination, and five minutes after we finally—*finally*—start convincing the public that we're not these radical nutjobs hell-bent on destroying society, another group that truly *is* pretty radical comes along and demands that we share all our hard-fought goodwill and legal victories with them.

"It's something I've been thinking about for a long time," Min was saying. "And I still don't know for sure. But I think I am. And since I started seeing Trai and Lena, I've decided it's at least something I want to explore."

This took another moment to sink in. Weirdly, it sounded familiar somehow.

"Wait," I said. "You really *are* coming out to me, aren't you?" *As polyamorous*, I thought.

"Are you freaked out?" Min asked me, her brown eyes boring into me.

I had to ask myself that question too. Was I freaked out?

Not really.

"I guess I'm disappointed you didn't feel like you could tell me this before," I said. But as soon as I said this, I realized I'd hated it when I'd come out to people as gay and they'd said those exact same words to me.

"It's not like that," Min said. "I wasn't sure I wanted to admit it to myself."

"Of course!" I said. "I know! That was a stupid thing for me to say. Forget I said it, okay?"

Min smiled. "Do you have questions?"

I did have questions. But since the first thing I'd said was totally dumb, I wasn't sure I wanted to risk saying more.

"How is being polyamorous different from just being slutty?" Min asked.

"No," I said, even though if I'm being honest, I was sort of thinking that.

"It's not about sex. Well, it is for some people. And that's okay. But for me, it was about getting closer and closer to both Trai and Lena. Suddenly it just didn't feel right to limit myself to one of them. I honestly think it's how I'm wired. I think that's the part that's like being gay."

I had to think about this, since she'd zeroed right in on that preexisting pet peeve of mine. But honestly, it did make a strange sort of sense. Not in the abstract—in Min's specific case. As long as I'd known her, she'd been drawn to new experiences. In high school, she'd taken AP Everything, and in college, she'd done a semester in Cameroon. She even seemed to like *people*. She wasn't like me, approaching every new person with complete suspicion—guilty until proven innocent. Nothing seemed to scare her either, not rejection, not being judged. She got right up in people's faces. Sometimes I think she even liked to shock people. And she was really competitive—that was part of her wiring too. It's why she'd argued with Gunnar about Bigfoot. Somehow the two things went hand-in-hand—being open to new ideas even as she was completely confident about her own.

Basically, Min had balls of brass.

"I can see it," I said.

"See what?" she said.

"That you're polyamorous. Or might be."

"How?"

I explained the part about how she was such an open, confident person, but I didn't use the expression "balls of brass" (one of things she gets up in people's faces about is the prevalence of sexism). I also left out the part about her being so competitive and liking to shock people, because, well, I try not to be a dick.

"You really think so?" she said.

I nodded.

"Are you wondering whether or not we get jealous?" Min said.

"What?" I said.

"Lena and Trai and I. That's what a lot of people think—that polyamorous relationships must be really hard because people get jealous. But it doesn't work like that."

"Min," I said. "You totally don't need to do the whole Poly 101 thing."

"I don't?"

I shook my head. "It's cool. I actually think it's great. Like I said, it makes a weird kind of sense. But even if it didn't, you're my friend. I'm happy you're happy."

She smiled. "I knew there was a reason I liked you. Now I want you to really get to know Lena and Trai. I really think you'll like them."

"I already like them."

"Oh, I hope to God you never have to lie to me for a good reason, like to save my life or something."

"I'm not—"

"Save it, please," Min said. "I know it's been awkward. I think they both felt really weird around you because I asked them to keep us a secret."

Could this be the truth? It actually made sense. It was nice to think that maybe they *didn't* hate me.

"When are you going to tell Gunnar?" I asked. Somehow I knew that she hadn't told him yet—that I'd be the one she'd tell first.

"Soon," she said. "But honestly, he's been so weird lately that I'm not sure it's the right time."

* * *

A few days after dinner with Kevin and Colin, Vernie asked me to go to a movie. I had a rare afternoon free, so we met at the Pacific Place—this downtown shopping mall with a gigantic glass atrium, and lots of high-end stores like Tiffany's and Ann Taylor. The movie theater is on the top balcony up near the atrium, so we had to ride the escalators up.

"So how *are* you?" Vernie said. It was still flattering that she was always so excited to see me. In my experience, old people react to people in their twenties in one of two ways: annoyance, like we're playing our music too loud, or condescension, like we're all just a bunch of lazy, self-absorbed idiots. (Wait, maybe it's three ways: old people are also constantly hitting on me in dating apps, so I guess they also want to fuck us.)

But Vernie wasn't like that. She actually seemed to *like* me—for who I was, I mean.

"Well, one of my best friends, Min, just came out to me as polyamorous," I said.

"She's a geometric shape?"

"It means she's drawn to more than one person at a time. Romantically."

"How is that different from every human being ever?"

I snorted. But then I actually thought about it: how *was* what Min had said different from everybody else?

"It's partly that they're more open about it," I said. "But it's different too. When they're *in* a relationship, they're not happy or satisfied with just one person."

"How is *that* different from every human being ever?"

I laughed again. But then I thought about this too. When I'd been with Kevin in high school, I'd been totally happy. (Or had I? I ended up breaking off the relationship after a couple of years, hadn't I? Besides, that was high school. Those relationships are different.)

"I'm only kidding," Vernie said. "I had some friends like that once when I lived in Los Angeles. 'Course they called it a 'group marriage' back then. Sadly, they were all a bunch of raving fruitcakes."

How long had Vernie been married anyway? Just as with her kids, she'd never talked about that. I was about to say something when we reached the top balcony. I started to step off, but I guess my shoe had been untied and the lace was stuck in the grating of the escalator. As the escalator rolled down, it pulled on my shoe.

"Damn it," I said, yanking on the lace, trying to pull it up. Inside the escalator, something made a quiet clicking sound.

Vernie stepped down on the lace, and the end popped free of the grate.

"Thanks," I said. I bent down to tie my shoe again.

"That's it!" Vernie said.

I looked up at her.

"I just saved your life," she said.

I just kept staring up at her.

"Don't you remember? I predicted I was going to save your life, and I just did. For the *second* time, I might add."

"You think it was going to pull me down into the escalator and grind me up?" I finished tying my shoe and stood up again.

"It could have."

"Come on."

166

"It could!"

"People don't die getting sucked into escalators."

"They do!" Vernie said. "All the time. If it hadn't been for me, you'd be hamburger right now."

"I'm looking it up on Snopes."

While we were in line to buy tickets, I actually did look it up on my phone, and to my surprise, there actually *are* a bunch of recorded cases of people getting their shoelaces stuck in escalators with pretty scary results. In the worst-case-scenarios, they try to get their laces free and end up with mangled fingers—although one guy supposedly got the strings to his hoodie stuck and strangled to death.

"Okay," I said at last. "I admit it was *theoretically* possible for me to have died. But the lace was barely stuck. That doesn't count as saving my life."

"Fine," Vernie said. "But you can buy your own damn popcorn!"

After the movie, Vernie said, "Let's get coffee and talk about it."

"Okay," I said. From the escalator going down, I looked around the mall. Weirdly, I only saw three coffee shops in direct view. Given this is Seattle, home to Starbucks, I would've expected at least six. But there were plenty of restaurants too.

"Not in here," she said. "Follow me."

So I followed her—outside, across the street, and down into the light rail station, where we caught a train to the south end of downtown.

"Where are we going?" I asked on the train.

"You'll see."

We got off at the Pioneer Square Station, and she led me up the hill, to the Columbia Center, which is, like, one of the tallest buildings in the world. (Wait. Go back. I just looked it up. It's not even in the top one hundred tallest buildings in the world. But it's still seventy-six stories tall, with another seven floors underground.)

"The Starbucks on the fortieth floor," I said to Vernie. I'd heard about it before, how there was this coffee shop in the "sky lobby" on the fortieth floor, and about what great views it had. It was a totally cheap way to see the city from high up without paying the twelve bucks it cost to go to the observation deck on the very top floor. I'd been meaning to come for years.

"Why just drink coffee when you can drink coffee at five hundred feet?" Vernie said. "It costs the same either way, correct?"

"Correct," I said. Knowing Vernie, this totally figured.

We rode the elevator up. Truthfully, I was a little disappointed. When you call something a "sky lobby," you're leading people to believe there will be massive art deco ceilings and soaring winged guardian-statues. But it turned out to be less *Bioshock: Infinite*'s city-in-the-clouds and more just a couple of hallways with several banks of elevators. That said, the corner view from the Starbucks was pretty great. Seattle is surrounded by water on three sides—Puget Sound to the west, Lake Union to the north, and Lake Washington to the east. From that coffee shop, you could see all three. And since the Columbia Center is the tallest building in town, on the fortieth floor you're already about as high up as most of the other skyscrapers.

As we were waiting in line to get our coffee, Vernie asked me, "So you didn't tell me how your date with Felicks went."

"Oh," I said, feeling awkward. "Well, he's a really nice guy. But his politics..."

"Politics?"

"He's a libertarian. Rand Paul supporter."

"Oh, good *God*." Her eyes bulged.

"Yeah, I know."

"I had no idea."

"Well, I still really appreciate you setting us up," I said. "I mean it. My parents...well, they've hardly ever even mentioned that I'm gay, not since I came out, like, six years ago. They never ask about my social life at all. I mean, it would probably be really horrible if they ever tried to set me up with a guy—I'd hate to see the kind of guy they'd want me to be with. But they'd never do it anyway, not in a million years. So it really means a lot that you did. It's like you're the mom I wish I'd had."

I said this without thinking, but as soon as it was out of my mouth, I regretted it. For one thing, it was weird to say while standing in line at Starbucks, even one in a "sky lobby." But for another thing, it seemed like I was putting Vernie in an awkward position. What if she didn't feel the same way?

"You're very sweet," she said.

That made me relax a little. But I couldn't help but notice that she turned forward in line and didn't say another word until after we'd both gotten our coffee from the barista.

* * *

We found a table at a window. Over on Puget Sound, a ferry was just heading off to Bainbridge Island. It was a quintessential Seattle scene, but I mostly ignored it. I sat there, waiting for my drink to cool—plain old drip coffee, Pike Place Roast (I hadn't wanted to assume Vernie was paying). Vernie didn't say anything either, just sipped her mocha Cookie Crumble Frappuccino with extra whipped cream.

Now I knew I'd offended her.

"You wanna know what happened to my kids," she said at last, not a question.

"Huh?" I said. "No. I wasn't going to ask that. That's none of my business."

"Maybe not," she said, "but you were wondering. Ever since it came up at dinner."

This was why Vernie had gotten so quiet? I hadn't offended her—I'd reminded her of her kids. I'd completely misread the situation, maybe the same way I'd done with Trai (but not with Colin).

"Yeah," I admitted. I *had* been wondering.

"There's no real mystery. I was a crappy mom. My kids hate me."

"Oh, I'm sure they don't—"

"Russel, it's okay. The paper lantern has already been torn off the light bulb on that one, okay? And, you know, they're right. I never wanted to be a mother in the first place, and I resented that they came between me and my writing. It wasn't just that either. I always had these *choices* to make. Either I could spend the weekend with Warren and Goldie, or I could go see my kid play soccer. Always these terrible choices. And I made the choices I did, but karma got her revenge. In the end, I was a bad mother, and I didn't get the writing career I wanted either. Although that also had to do with sexism—it wasn't *all* my fault."

"I'm sorry," I said, even as I was also thinking, *You got invited to spend weekends with Warren Beatty and Goldie Hawn?*

Vernie tugged an ear. "It is what it is. I made the choices, I have to live with the consequences. Everything in life has a price. But I haven't given up on my kids completely. I have this idea that there'll be a big happy reunion in the end. In the movie of my life, there sure would be." She sipped her drink. It left a small whipped cream Hitler mustache, but only until she licked her lip. "But enough about you, let's talk about me, right? What'd you think of the movie?"

What did I think of what? It was strange to shift gears so rapidly.

"I'm sorry," Vernie said. "I don't like to talk about it. I've made a lot of mistakes in my life—we all have. But screwing up your job as a parent? That's one of the mistakes that most people think is unforgiveable. And they're right—it *is* unforgiveable. I have no excuse for what I did, except I'm a bad person."

"I hated it," I said.

Vernie's eyes met mine, and she smiled as broadly as I'd seen her smile all day, and I knew I'd played it exactly right. The kind thing to do here wasn't to say, "No! You're really a great person!" but to simply let her have her moment of grief and move on.

But at the same time, I couldn't help but wonder if the fact that she'd taken an interest in me in the first place didn't have something to do with her own kids, if I was somehow sort of giving her a chance to "do over" her parenting. I mean, duh, right? It was funny how people really did make at least a tiny bit more sense when you stopped seeing them from just your own point of view and started thinking about how they might see themselves.

"What did you hate about it?" Vernie asked me.

"Well, it looked great," I said. "And it was well-acted. But I hated the characters." We'd gone to see this arthouse movie that had been getting really good reviews. It was called *Midnight Calling*, and it was about this guy and girl who agree to pretend to be a drug dealer and a prostitute in order to save someone's life. But as the night goes on, they discover they really like it, and they have no interest in going back to their old, boring lives.

"So you think characters have to be likable for a movie to be good?"

"No," I said. "Obviously not."

"Why is that obvious?"

"Because there are a lot of great movie characters who aren't likeable at all."

"Like who?"

"I don't know. Norman Bates."

"You've seen *Psycho*?"

"Sure." I was happy she was impressed, which is why I didn't mention that I totally didn't get what the big deal was about the shower scene. (Yes, yes, it was revolutionary at the time. I'm not an idiot.)

"But even if they're not likeable, characters still have to be interesting," I said. "The characters in that movie were pretty much just, well, assholes." I was a little embarrassed to use that word in front of Vernie, being an old person and all, but I knew she wouldn't be offended, that she sometimes even swore herself.

"I get that your characters have to be flawed—that if they're too perfect they're boring. But I've never understood why people think just being an asshole makes you interesting—in books and movies, I mean. There are enough assholes in real life—why would I want to spend time with them in the movies? There has to be a really good reason."

"Well, interesting characters are a lot harder to write than they look," Vernie said. "And of course 'asshole' is in the eye of the beholder. But I've thought the same thing. For a long time, the leading characters in movies *had* to be saintly. There was even a code. But now we've gone too far in the other direction. It's like the more an asshole a character is, the more it's an indication of the writer's 'bravery' and 'authenticity.' I think it has to do with the rise of the counter-culture in the sixties and seventies. The 'hero' became someone who questioned authority, someone who stood up against the prevailing culture. But then the counter-culture *became* the culture. Which was actually pretty great until the corporations started using counter-culture attitudes to sell shoes and music and soda pop. And then the conservatives co-opted it to sell wars and tax cuts for millionaires. Then came the rise of irony, and a corresponding rise in cynicism, and eventually it all collapsed into nihilism. Now we're condemned to sit through a bunch of movies where no one cares about anything except themselves, and they tell us it's all so revolutionary and daring, when it's really just the same old pandering."

"Yeah," I said. I wasn't used to feeling stupid around people, not even Min. But right then, I felt stupid around Vernie.

"The feeling I get these days," Vernie said, "is that

a lot of writers don't like their characters very much. Or maybe it's that they don't like the audience. All I know is it has something to do with how they feel, which isn't good. I suppose it all comes back to their view of human nature. Is there anything redeemable about us at all?"

"What do you think?" I said.

She thought for a second. "I think that as a species, we're cruel, small-minded, bigoted, superstitious, completely self-centered, and incredibly short-sighted. But that there are still plenty of individuals among us, maybe ten percent, who are simply grand. Present company included."

I smiled. "And those are the characters you write about?"

"You bet your boots." She slurped her coffee. "What's your view of human nature?"

"What you said sounds about right."

"No, really. Tell me."

I had to think, not just because I wanted to impress Vernie, but also because I wanted to tell the truth. I sipped my coffee now too. It was finally cool enough to drink. And if it acted like most hot beverages, it would stay just the right temperature for about thirty seconds.

"People mostly suck," I said. "But sometimes they surprise you."

"Oh!" Vernie said, grinning. "That's much better than what I said. Much more concise."

Vernie's reaction made me feel warm inside. It was even better than coffee at the right temperature.

"What's sad," Vernie said, "is that these days, we're what passes for optimists."

I guffawed. "What was it like, working as a screenwriter in Hollywood?"

"Complicated. There are three main forces behind every movie, all very, very powerful. There's the producer, or whoever has the money. He's the most powerful force of all—and I'm not being sexist when I say 'he.' One way or another, it's always a he. Then there's the director, who also has a lot of power. And for what it's worth, that's almost always a 'he' too. Then there are the actors—the bigger the actor is, the more powerful they are. If they're really big, they might even have more clout than the director. But probably not the producer, at least not if he's also the financier. One way or another, those three forces need to be in synch, even if it's some kind of competitive rivalry. If they're not...well, have you ever wondered why there are so many crappy movies?"

"Wait," I said. "What about the screenwriter?"

"What about her?" Vernie said.

"Well, isn't she one of the main forces too?" I made a point to use "she" for Vernie's benefit.

"Oh, you dear sweet boy."

"What?"

"Screenwriters don't have any power in Hollywood. Absolutely none. We're the lowest of the low, at least once we've signed the contract. They ignore you, fire you, rewrite you. In Hollywood, you actually have to have them write it into your contract that they invite you to the premiere, because otherwise they won't. The writer is just that much of an afterthought."

"But if not for the writer, there wouldn't even be a movie in the first place."

"You're preaching to the choir, Chickadee. But that's not the way they see it. It's just not. Which isn't really funny, because the writer is the one person who's most concerned with story—the person who wants it to all hang together. To have a point. Not a point-point, like a lecture, but an *emotional* point. To have an ending that's totally unexpected, yet completely inevitable."

"What does that mean?"

She thought for a second. "A screenplay needs to build. Everything is there for a reason, and the reason is usually the ending. It makes everything that came before it make sense. But at the same time, it can't be predictable or it'll be boring. So the writer has to be one step ahead of the audience—she has to give them something fresh and different and unexpected. Or she can rely on gimmicks—clever slang, or explosions, or chase scenes, or gratuitous sex. Being shocking in some new way works too." She gave me an exaggerated once-over. "You should be writing this down—this is good stuff!"

I smiled, but part of me knew she was telling the truth. "It sounds like it was also hard to be a woman."

"Are you kidding? Hollywood is the town that finally figured out a way to make romantic comedies without women—with only straight men. All those 'bromance' movies a few years back? I couldn't believe it. Or that Muppets movie reboot not long ago? There are something like twenty-five male Muppets and two female ones. The rebooted movie made a big deal about adding a brand new Muppet. So who was it? Of course it was another male. And the really weird thing was, no one even noticed. No one said one word. And you're thinking, 'It's just the

Muppets, so what?' But imagine a children's movie with twenty-five female characters and two male ones. Or *any* movie. How do you think men would react to that kind of casual indifference?"

I raised an eyebrow. I hadn't thought about Hollywood like that before, but I couldn't really disagree.

"It's not that the men in Hollywood are bad people—some of them are perfectly fine, very decent. They just only ever see things *their* way, from *their* perspective. They claim they're in charge because they know how to make the money. Well, the big irony is that having more diverse voices in Hollywood would actually make them *more* money. But they'd also have to give up control, they'd have to give someone else access to the cash, and *that's* not going to happen any time soon. Take the movie today. A woman whose secret desire is to be a prostitute? That's really what they think women wanna see? For the six hundred zillionth time?"

"So you didn't like it either?"

"The movie? I agreed with every single word you said before."

"But it's getting such good reviews."

"Well, keep in mind that I'm the writer who thought that *Pretty Woman* shouldn't be a romantic fantasy. I have no idea what I'm talking about. After all, nobody knows anything."

"They don't?"

"That's a famous quote by a screenwriter named William Goldman. He said that about Hollywood— 'nobody knows anything.' He meant that everyone talks like screenwriting is a science, that there's some rhyme and reason to the business of making movies. But there really isn't. No one knows beforehand what the audience is going to respond to. But I've always thought it applied to *everything* about screenwriting. Everyone always talks like they're experts, like they know what the hell they're talking about. I did, just now. But we're all winging it, making it up as we go along. Some of us are just a lot better at sounding confident. Or we're too stupid to realize that art is all opinion. Completely subjective."

"That's kind of scary," I said.

"Is it? I think it's liberating. We do our best, sometimes it works and sometimes it doesn't, and then we move on."

Was Vernie talking about her kids again? I wasn't sure, but I decided not to chance it, even though I'd been waiting for an opportunity to ask her about her weekends with Warren and Goldie.

I sipped my coffee. Sure enough, it was already lukewarm, and I hadn't even drunk half. But I was having a good time, and I didn't want this coffee date to end. So I said, "Did you like it? Working in Hollywood?"

Vernie turned and looked out the window. In the building across from us, someone was sitting at a window drinking coffee and staring over at us. Down on Elliott Bay, a second ferry was leaving, to Bremerton this time.

When Vernie didn't say anything, I looked back at her. She wasn't looking out at downtown Seattle anymore—she was back to staring at me, her lips twitching now.

"What?" I said. It was like she'd been whispered the most delightful secret.

"Working in Hollywood was annoying, frustrating, depressing, taxing, infuriating, and completely soul-deadening." She hesitated for the perfect amount of time and gave me another one of her trademark grins. "And I absolutely loved every minute of it!"

CHAPTER TWELVE

That weekend, Gunnar was visiting his parents, so I decided to catch a ride down with him on Saturday morning and stay with my own parents for the night. I'd have to take a bus back home Sunday morning in order to get to my job at Green Lake by noon, but it had been a while since I'd seen my parents, and I knew they'd be happy to see me.

Besides, there was something to be said for getting out of the rut where my life was basically alternating between going to work and obsessing about Kevin. I also figured it would give me a chance to spend some quality time with Gunnar. His and my hometown—the place where we went to high school together—is about an hour south of Seattle, so we had lots of time to talk.

"Grover Krantz was one of the only traditional scientists to take the study of Bigfoot seriously," Gunnar said at one point. "He died in 2002, but he spent a lot of his career studying Bigfoot footprints, casts and stuff like that. Most of them were hoaxes, but he was convinced that some of them would have been almost impossible to fake—that they'd require an incredible knowledge of human anatomy and physical design. For example, the Bossburg casts show evidence of a foot with an old bone injury. And also spreading of the toes. Krantz theorized that Bigfoot might be an undiscovered remnant population of a species of giant ape that was thought to have gone extinct three hundred thousand years ago—the largest ape that ever lived. They lived in Asia, but Krantz said they could have crossed over on the Bering Land Bridge that was later used by humans to populate North America."

So much for spending quality time with Gunnar, I thought.

I'd never been annoyed by Gunnar's obsessions before—not seriously annoyed. On the contrary, they were one of the things that made me like him. So why did this stupid Bigfoot thing feel so different? Was it just because I was discovering that I didn't have any real passions in my own life—or anything that I even really cared all that much about? Was I jealous?

When we got close to town, I said, "Why don't we just go straight to your house?" It was only about a fifteen minute walk from his parents' house to mine, and I figured it would be nice to see the old neighborhood. "Besides, then I can stop in and say hi to your parents."

"Nah," Gunnar said. "I'll drive you home."

"It's okay, I'm actually looking forward—"

"I'll take you home!" Gunnar said, and I looked at his white knuckles as he clenched the steering wheel.

I decided then and there that whatever the hell was going on with him, it was a remnant population of giant apes that I had no interest in disturbing.

It's a cliché to come home to your childhood house, look at your bedroom, and realize how much you've changed. But it's a cliché for a reason. People grow up and become different. But assuming you move out of the house at some point, which not all people my age do, your bedroom doesn't change. It stays the same, exactly the way you were in high school. It's like this wormhole to the past.

I stared around the room, at my swimming trophies and my collection of plastic collectibles from animated Disney movies. In the shelf on the bottom of the bedstand was a book, *Eight Plays* by Tennessee Williams. I'd found it on my parents' bookshelves my freshman year in high school. I have no idea why I'd started reading it—had I heard somewhere that the playwright was gay? But I'd loved it. It had all of his most famous plays—*Cat on a Hot Tin Roof*, *Summer and Smoke*, *Sweet Bird of Youth*, and, yes, *A Streetcar Named Desire*. But the one I liked the most (by far) was *The Glass Menagerie*. It struck me as the gayest thing ever written, even though it never once says the word "gay." And it isn't gay because Amanda is campy, or because the metaphor of Laura's delicate, fragile glass menagerie is so romantic and beautiful. It's because of the narrator, Tom.

Tom is telling the audience a story from his past, something that clearly still haunts him. It turns out to be about his overbearing mother, Amanda, and Laura, his timid dreamer of a sister. Tom wants to be a writer, but he has to work at a job he hates in order to support his mother and sister. But over the course of the play, it becomes clear that Tom is also gay (although this is never stated outright—that's sort of the whole point, that it *can't* be stated outright, especially not in the 1930s when the play is set). Tom resents that he can't be himself, and also how much his mother and sister rely on him—they're too damaged and delusional to survive on their own. In the end (spoiler alert!), he grows so stifled and frustrated that he just leaves, even though he knows it will destroy them both. Just like the glass menagerie, the illusions of Amanda and Laura and even Tom are too fragile to survive, so everything breaks. But afterward Tom feels so guilty about what he's done that it basically destroys him too.

I later learned that Tennessee Williams' real name was Tom, and that he had a sister like Laura who was eventually institutionalized, and a mom like Amanda, and that he was a tortured alcoholic. Which makes perfect sense. Tennessee Williams' other plays have bigger themes and are more ambitious—especially *A Streetcar Named Desire*. But before *The Glass Menagerie*, I'd never before read anything that felt so personal (I still haven't). It was like Tennessee Williams was inviting you into his deepest, most personal, most painful memory. Was Tom an asshole? Well, yeah, I guess, maybe, depending on your point of view. But it's mostly just stupid to ask the question, because the whole play seems so real and heartbreaking and sad. It's impossible to judge Tom (or Amanda, or Laura), because you totally understand them, and they're caught in an impossible situation with no good choices, and they're all doing the best they can to survive. The play doesn't have a fake, feel-good happy ending like *Pretty Woman*. You know in your gut the story has to end exactly the way it does.

Maybe this was what Vernie meant about how a good ending to a story is both completely inevitable and yet somehow still totally surprising.

Later, my parents took me out to dinner at the golf club. My parents aren't particularly rich, and they don't actually play golf—they're just "social" members of the club, so my mom can play in the bridge tournament, and we can eat in the restaurant. Which tells you a lot about my parents—basically, that they care a whole lot about social status (especially my mom). This came into play big-time when they learned about my being gay, especially since it was 2007, before most of Middle America had decided being gay *wasn't* actually a Big Screaming Deal That Makes Your Head Explode.

For a sixteen-year-old, this was traumatic, and I confess I was still a little bitter, even seven years later. My parents met Kevin Land a few times, but they never even knew he and I were together (they never asked, and I never told). I'd never brought a boy-friend home from college either, mostly because my parents never asked if I had one.

I used to say that all I had in common with my parents was a house and some DNA. But now there wasn't even the house.

On the other hand, DNA isn't nothing. Neither is the fact that they loved me. And I loved them. My parents were good people. Like Tom and Amanda and Laura, they were just doing the best they could under the circumstances.

The point is, it was actually nice to see them.

"So, Russel," my dad said, slurping his chowder at the golf club restaurant. "How's life?"

I thought about the question, about how much truth I could tell my parents without turning their world upside down. That I'd thought I'd had a new fuck buddy in the form of Boston, the hot mechanic, but then he'd told me he was on PrEP and so he wanted to start barebacking? Um, no, that was out. The fact that my bisexual best friend Min had recently come out to me as possibly polyamorous, and that she was currently dating both a guy and a girl? No, I was pretty sure that was out too.

"Good," I said, nodding to the waiter that yes, I wanted ground pepper on my salad. "It's going good."

"'Well'," my mom said. She was correcting my grammar—it was going "well" in my life, which is grammatically correct, not "good." She'd been an English major in college.

I just smiled, doing everything I could not to grab that pepper grinder and jam it down her throat. Suddenly it was *extremely* hard to remember that she was just doing the best she could under the circumstances. Seriously, is there anything more off-putting than someone correcting your grammar? Vernie never did that.

But that reminded me of something. I said, "I saved someone from drowning at Green Lake."

"Really?" my mom said. "That's fantastic. Tell us all about it."

And so I did. Until I got to the part where Vernie

invited me over to her house for dinner, and I'd gone alone, and she'd told me that my drink was a whiskey sour, and how I'd decided she wasn't Stifler's Mom, but more like Kathy Griffin, except better. Somehow I didn't think they'd understand any of that either.

My parents smiled and nodded and congratulated me, and then they went on talking about their lives, about how my mom's book club was reading *Water For Elephants*, and about how my dad's new office had been built with some European design that was supposed to keep it warm in the winter and cool in the summer, but that the architect had failed to account for all the computer monitors, so now they had to install air conditioners.

Were they telling *me* the whole truth about their lives? Did they have anything they couldn't share with me, for fear that I couldn't really handle or understand it, the way I did with them? You can't ever be certain about the private lives of other people—hey, maybe my parents were swingers, and they'd never gotten up the nerve to tell me.

I doubted it. I think I understood my parents pretty well, their faults, their strengths, but mostly their real selves—or as "real" as anyone ever is. If our family life was a play, I'd already sat through thousands of performances, and I knew all the subtext.

But just like Amanda and Laura didn't know Tom, not really, my parents didn't know me—maybe not at all. Yeah, I know that's what every kid thinks about his or her parents—that's what kids have *always* thought about their parents, and a lot of them are wrong, because adults aren't as clueless as you think. (Sadly, mine are.)

But that's not even the part I was focusing on as we had our soup and salad course in that restaurant at the golf club. It was more about how different their lives were from mine—how different they must have been even when they were my age.

My dad was an accountant. His dad was an accountant too, and he'd gone to school in order to take on the family business. Did my dad resent that? Probably a little. But he'd done it. And if I'd had to guess, knowing my dad the way I thought I did, I'd say he never really thought about it all that much. There had been a pathway laid out for him—a level, paved pathway lined with fashionable recessed lighting and well-trimmed shrubbery—and he'd taken it. And he loved my mom—I never doubted that either.

Meanwhile, my mom loved my dad. And she seemed to like her job as an office manager. If I'd had to guess, I'd say she'd liked raising me too—at least until her precious son had come out as gay, which had admittedly been a big meteor in the middle of her own shrubbery-lined pathway.

Did my parents have Unstoppable Career Drive or Passionate Aimlessness? Even asking the question about them seemed sort of ridiculous. Maybe things were different when they were in their twenties (of course they were). They had to have asked *some* of the same questions I'd been asking myself. They'd just answered them already, so there was no point in asking them anymore. Vernie had told me that people had *always* wrestled with these same questions. And I definitely don't want to say that my parents' lives were easier than mine. Who knew what struggles they went through? I know my mom had problems with anxiety (she took Xanax), and my dad had these migrating skin rashes.

But things *did* seem different now, and not just because of gay people, and fuck buddies, and polyamorous triads. These days, it seemed like everyone my age wanted to be Outrageously Happy, not Merely Content (like the previous generation). Which was ironic, because so much in life—a decent education, a reasonably good job, a nice house—seemed so much harder than it had been for the generation before.

Needless to say, I wasn't Outrageously Happy. I wasn't even Merely Content. And the really scary thing was, I was starting to think I never would be.

When we got home from dinner that night, I had planned on watching some TV in my bedroom. I'd been binge-watching old episodes of *Supernatural* on Netflix. (Who is hotter, Jensen Ackles or Jared Padalecki? The age-old debate continues!)

But then I checked Facebook and happened to see a post from Kevin. After we'd reconnected, I'd un-unfriended him, and I forgotten to unfriend him again (un-un-unfriend?).

Visiting the parents for the weekend. Hi, Mom! (Yes, she's a Facebook friend.)

This was a coincidence: Kevin had come home for the weekend too. Like Gunnar, he didn't live very far from me. I couldn't help but wonder if he'd brought Colin with him.

I decided to hell with Jensen and Jared, that I'd go for a walk. I'd wanted to go for a walk around town earlier, but Gunnar hadn't let me, remember? True, it was too dark to see much, but still. I wasn't going to walk by Kevin's house and try to glance in the window or anything stalker-y like that. Besides, Kevin had made it very clear he didn't want to see me, even though we were supposedly "really, really good friends"—not for "a while."

I walked to this park near my house. It wasn't anywhere near Kevin's, although I admit it was between our houses, about halfway. Since it was after dark, the park was completely deserted. In the back of the park, behind the play area and the tennis courts, there's this little picnic gazebo. But the park is built up against a green belt, and there's a swamp in those woods, and the smell is just incredibly foul—really sulfur-y from the rotting weeds and stagnant water. So no one ever actually uses the gazebo, not even during the day. This was actually the place that Kevin and I used to meet in high school, back when we first started seeing each other. It had been perfect, precisely because it always *was* so deserted. In fact, it was the first place we *ever* met, before we even knew each other's real names, after we'd met in an online chat room. We hadn't done anything there that first night, sexually I mean, but we had later.

I posted to my own Facebook page.

Back home for the weekend, out for a walk.

And I took a picture of the stinky picnic gazebo and posted it. The photo was dark—the closest light was over by the tennis courts—but if you looked hard, you could still make it out.

I know what you're thinking: I was doing all this because I wanted Kevin to see it and come and meet me here. And, yeah, okay, maybe you're right. This wasn't why I'd come back to visit my parents—I hadn't even known Kevin would be in town. But now that we both happened to be there, I couldn't help but think about what Min had said, that Colin was jealous of me—and that maybe he had a *reason* to be jealous. That Kevin had admitted to Colin his feelings for me, or maybe Colin had just sensed them somehow.

So I guess I was testing Kevin, trying to find out if any of that was true. He'd said he was in love with Colin, that his feelings for me were different now. Was *that* true? It's not like I was forcing him to come meet me.

So I waited. It was summer, and the air was perfect, not too warm and not too cold. Unfortunately, the smell from the swamp was as bad as ever. It had been different before, whenever I'd come to meet Kevin. Then I hadn't ever minded the smell. (In fact, for a long time after, I'd start to get a boner every time I smelled rotten eggs.)

Something buzzed over in the swamp, and frogs croaked too. But nothing was moving, not the slightest bit. The greenbelt was a tangled smear of grey foliage, not a single leaf fluttering. Fir trees towered out of the undergrowth, tapering upward, straight, unbending, their uppermost tips almost reaching the haze of mist that hung frozen in the sky, seemingly just above them. I couldn't see the water in the swamp, but somehow I could *feel* it—stagnant, un-moving, choked with algae. Even the air seemed still. It felt like time had stopped, like I'd stepped into a photograph (a decent one, not the crappy one I'd posted on Facebook).

Something finally moved in the night, a dark figure approaching—somehow both tentative and confi-dent. It was either a serial killer or Kevin, and I wasn't sure which was making me shake more.

Slowly, the shadowy figure coalesced into You Know Who.

"*Kevin?*" I said, appropriately shocked. "What are you doing here?" Then, probably pushing it a little too far, I said, "I didn't even know you were in town."

"I saw your post," he said. He hesitated. "I thought maybe you saw my post, and you wanted me to see yours too."

"No," I said in possibly the most unconvincing lie of all time. "That's not it at all."

He stopped about ten feet in front of me. I could just barely make out his face, but it looked blotchy and mottled in the moonlight—a half-finished sculp-ture made of grey clay. There must have been subtle-ties there, all kinds of nuance, but I couldn't see it, and the closely-cropped beard wasn't helping.

We both stood there, staring at each other in the dark, neither of us moving. At least I'd managed to stop myself from shaking.

"This was a mistake," he said at last. "I shouldn't have come." But I couldn't help but notice that he didn't turn to leave.

"Why *did* you come?" I said. The second part of that question went unspoken: *You said you didn't want to see me for "a while."* What had he meant by "a while" anyway? At the time, it had seemed like more than a week and a half.

"Why did you post that picture on Facebook?" Kevin said.

Suddenly he and I were playing a game of nine-dimensional chess.

"To see if you'd come," I admitted. "And you did. Now tell me why."

"I don't know," he said. "Because I'm stupid."

"You said you're in love with Colin."

"I am."

"And you said you didn't want to see me."

"I don't."

Really? I thought.

"Colin's an asshole," I said. "You know that, right?"

Kevin's face shifted, but I still couldn't make it out in the moonlight. "He was to you. But I would be too, if I thought he still had feelings for someone else."

"Do you?" I said. "Do you still have feelings for me? You said we were just friends."

Just say it, I thought. *You owe me that.*

But he didn't say it. Instead, he stepped closer, so close I could finally smell him, even over the swamp. Back in high school, he'd used to smell like dollar soap and leather from his baseball mitt. He didn't smell like that now. He was wearing cologne, and I could also smell his brand of designer soap, but those weren't what I noticed. It was the scent of something hairy and wild, but this was no Bigfoot. No, Kevin was definitely a man.

His face was clearer now, not mottled by the dark, but it was still confusing. Or maybe there was just too much subtlety for me to process, too many mixed emotions.

He moved to kiss me. His teeth glowed white in the moonlight.

This wasn't what I had planned. Or maybe I hadn't thought this far ahead. In retrospect, it was obvious that this was the only way this night could have ended—inevitable and surprising, at least to me.

And yet, the scene didn't end. The story wasn't over yet.

What about Colin? I wanted to say. I was *going* to say it. But I didn't. I didn't want to know the answer anyway.

We were kissing now, and I was feeling his beard against my face, scratching a deep itch I hadn't known I had. He tasted like he smelled—wild, a mountain river running free after a spring melt. My tongue touched his teeth, those clean white tabs. He was opening his mouth for me, soft and wet and wonderful, and I was opening for him too. I could feel the little gusts from his nose on my cheek, warm and heady.

My hands were on him, all over him, feeling his waist, his arms, his torso, his back, and down. He felt so familiar, so much like he had in high school. But he felt different too—broader at the shoulders, a little thicker around the torso, but just as trim about the waist.

He'd been a teenager before—admittedly, one with a five o'clock shadow by ten in the morning. But now he was a man, undeniably so.

We both were. We were two grown men, alone in the moonlight shadow of that gazebo. There was nothing tentative about the way we were now, not like when we'd been teenagers, excited, but timid and bashful and afraid.

Our clothes started coming off. No one could see, not in the emptiness near the stinky picnic gazebo, but I wouldn't have cared even if they did. I shucked off my sweatshirt and t-shirt together, like I was a knight flinging away my armor after a victorious battle. Was that what this was? Had I vanquished Colin? But for the time being, it was the thought of Colin I most wanted to vanquish.

Kevin was wearing a sweatshirt too, and a dark t-shirt underneath, and they came off in the swirl of a tornado. As they flew to one side, I caught another whiff of his body—not his sweat exactly, but his scent. Masculine.

Kevin had always had a hairy chest, and it was thicker now, but not unruly. It wasn't out of control like Ben and the other Bigfoot hunters, but he wasn't waxed and shaved like a lot of gay guys either. It was just trimmed like the hair on his face. He hadn't known how incredibly hot he was in high school, not really. We'd both been tentative and scared and fumbling. Neither of us had really known what it was like to have sex appeal, that guys could even *be* sexy, at least to each other. Kevin and I had discovered all that together, and we'd studied hard, but we'd never graduated, never gone beyond the 100 level.

We both knew it now, that we were sexy, that we could be attractive to men—even hot men like Felicks and Boston and Colin. Kevin had something to offer, something sensual, something other men wanted. But I did too. I didn't have *a* passion in my life, but I still had passion, at least when I was with another man.

And I could *inspire* passion too. I no longer had any doubt of that.

I stared at Kevin in the dark. I could see his face more clearly now, his lips, the angle of his jaw, even his white teeth when he smiled, but I still couldn't see his eyes, not in the shadowy recesses of his face, and I knew he couldn't see mine.

I didn't care. This was something different from before, from what we had in high school, what we'd done then. That was sweet, innocent. This was something more primal, more urgent—more dangerous.

Then we were both marching in place, stepping out of our pants, underwear and all—unabashed, confident. Kevin was hard, just like I knew he would be, just like he'd always been when we'd met before like this. It stood upright, arced and barely even bobbing, even as he kicked off his pants. It rose up from a pair of tight balls and a thick patch of dark hair—maybe he trimmed that too, but no mere razor was a match for all that testosterone. Kevin's dick was familiar, like I remembered, but somehow different too—a vein I didn't recall, a sharper glans.

It throbbed, and moonlight glinted on the moisture that welled from the tip.

Then we were kissing again, wet and messy. We thrust our bodies together, already sweaty, both of our dicks leaking something bad, making sticky streaks across our stomachs. Nothing in that park had been moving before, but now everything was, all around me. The dense foliage rippled in the force of an invisible breeze, leaves rustling, one thatch entwining with together, merging together. The waters in the swamp surged and oozed, dripping, thick with algae,

warm and slippery to the touch. And more than anything, the tapered fir trees stretched ever higher,
impossibly tall, stiff, straining their roots, desperate to
slip inside the wiry clouds delicately teasing their tips.

Oh, fuck it! Enough with the metaphors! Kevin
and I were both rock hard and desperate to fuck. I
wanted to be inside him, to feel all of him from the
inside out, and then to have him inside me, deeper
than he'd ever been—deeper than *anyone* had ever
been.

"Do you...?"

"Yeah," I breathed. "In my pocket." I'd brought
condoms—four of them, one for each of us to fuck
the other, maybe even more than once—and even a
not-so-little packet of lube. And that pretty much
gave up the ghost that my Facebook post had been
anything other than a blatant attempt to get into
Kevin's pants. I lied before, to myself especially, when
I'd said I hadn't expected this, that I hadn't seen it
coming. It's what I'd wanted all along, what I was
determined to get. It's not only that I wanted to fuck
him, and wanted him to fuck me. I wanted what it all
meant—that he still loved me, that he loved me more
than Colin, that he wanted me back.

I was on him first, just the way I wanted it—
controlling him, controlling the whole night. The
swamp and the foliage and the trees were back to
being still, frozen, or maybe they were shocked and
breathless by what they were seeing in front of them,
by what we were doing. But I didn't stop, not for a
second. I reveled in it, taking him from behind,
sliding into an impossible squeeze, forcefully, causing
a sharp gasp, one I'm not sure came from him or me.

Maybe it was both of us together, surrendering to the need.

And on I went, slamming forward, unstoppable. I owned this night, just like I now owned Kevin, and there was nothing, no force in the world, that could keep me from burying myself deep inside them both.

CHAPTER THIRTEEN

Later, things returned to normal. Nothing was different, and everything was. Someday some scientist is going to win a Nobel Prize by proving that orgasms don't just change a person's perception—they literally alter reality. Count on it.

Kevin and I were lying on our backs on the grass near the picnic gazebo, side by side, still gasping for air, the perspiration slowly cooling on our skin. The evidence of what we'd done was all around us, was undeniable. It wasn't just our naked bodies, both our cocks still wet and slick and slowly deflating. It was the piles of discarded clothes thrown haphazardly around. And then there were the two used condoms, rumpled and twisted along the tops of the grass like discarded snakeskins.

What have I done? I thought.

I sat upright. "Are you okay?"

"It's all good," Kevin said quietly.

But it wasn't all good. Nothing was good.

Kevin didn't move, but I did. I crawled toward the piles of clothing, searching for my underwear. I found my boxer briefs and slipped them on, and that made me feel better somehow. Kevin still hadn't moved, just laid there on his back, naked, even though his breathing had finally returning to normal. Somehow it seemed dick-y to put the rest of my clothes back on, so I didn't. I crawled back over toward him and sat back on the grass again.

"I'm sorry," I said.

"It wasn't your fault," he said.

We both stared up at the thick haze. Had there been stars before? There weren't any now. Had I *ever* been able to see the stars from this park with all the lights of the city? I suddenly couldn't remember.

I looked to one side, only to be confronted by those two condoms again—both surprisingly full of thick white liquid.

Two condoms. I'd fucked Kevin first, and I'd come. Then he'd fucked me. Which meant I'd kept going, kept having sex with him even after I'd come. I tried to tell myself that, well, I was being a decent guy, not just getting off and wanting to stop, not caring about his getting off too. But that's not what it was. I'd *wanted* to keep going. I'd *wanted* Kevin to fuck me—not because I was turned on (I'd just come), or because I especially like getting fucked (I don't).

It was because I'd wanted Kevin to want me. Which meant that, weirdly, this whole encounter hadn't really had all that much to do with sex, at least on my part. I'd been lying to myself (again) when I'd said that my having an orgasm had changed every-thing. It hadn't really changed anything.

And Kevin *had* wanted me. I'd been right all along. Kevin still loved me—so much he was willing to betray Colin for me.

So why didn't that feel good? I'd won. I'd gotten exactly what I'd wanted, what I'd planned.

I don't think I'd ever felt worse in my life. It felt like someone had poured fresh concrete into my soul, wet and heavy, full of ground-up rocks. Even now, I tried to tell myself that I was like Tom in *The Glass Menagerie*, that my actions were completely understandable given the circumstances—that it was impossible to judge me.

But that was yet another lie. I was like the characters in *Midnight Calling*, that movie Vernie and I had both hated. Seducing an ex because you're lonely and insecure, and you want to get revenge on his jerk of a boyfriend? That made me just another asshole.

There was a garbage can over by the picnic gazebo, so I stood up, grabbed both the condoms, and dropped them into the trash.

It didn't help. Even with the condoms out of sight, I didn't feel any better.

Here we go, I thought. I guess I was like Tom in *The Glass Menagerie* in one way: I was now going to be haunted by what I'd done.

I returned to Kevin and sat back on the grass. "So now what?" I said.

He sat upright at last, hugging his legs with his arms. "Who knows?"

"When are you going to tell Colin?"

He looked at me. His face had been a lump of clay before, too hard or too complicated to make out, but it wasn't now. He was looking at me like I was batshit crazy.

Then he looked scared.

"You're not going to tell him, are you?" he said.

"No," I said. "Of course not. But..."

"What?"

"What about us?"

"I don't know. I need time to think. This is all so crazy." He stood up and walked to his clothes. He didn't have any problem putting everything on even though I was still mostly undressed—not just his underwear, but his pants, his t-shirt, his sweatshirt. At least he kept his socks and shoes off.

He came back and sat down next to me. "I'm sorry," he said. "We'll figure this out. Okay? I just need some time. Colin is gone all next weekend at a conference. Do you wanna come over? We can get some dinner and talk."

And fuck, I thought. And even now, post-orgasm, the idea excited me.

"But you're going to tell Colin, right? Soon?"

Kevin stood up again, suddenly, and turned away from me. "Russel! Can we just not make any decisions right now? This is all pretty sudden, you know."

"So...what?" I said. "We're having some kind of affair?" Of course we were having an affair. What else would you call it? Then I had a hopeful thought. "I don't suppose you and Colin have an open relationship...?" This hadn't even occurred to me before, but if they did, it meant I hadn't done anything wrong. Didn't it?

But Kevin quickly snatched the paper lantern off *that* light bulb. He looked down at me like I was batshit crazy again.

"Okay, fine," I said. "But I'd still like to know what this means."

"I don't know what it means. Like I said, can we just not make any decisions right now?"

"But—"

"Look! You wanted me to come here tonight. You had this whole thing planned right from the start."

"I posted a picture on Facebook," I said. "It's not like I'm this master manipulator—Kevin Spacey in fucking *House of Cards*."

"Still. You brought condoms. You planned this."

Busted.

But I said, "Not *this*. Although right now I'm not even sure what 'this' is."

This was all so ironic. I thought I'd been so clever, seducing Kevin, vanquishing Colin. And if the price I had to pay was some guilty feelings, a tortured *Glass Menagerie*-like haunting for a few months, well, maybe it would have been worth it, because at least I would've had Kevin back. But it sounds like I *didn't* have Kevin back. I'd "had" him, for about twenty minutes (okay, thirty-five), but now he was saying he didn't want to make any decisions right now. How different was that from him saying that we were "really, really good friends"?

I made the choices, Vernie had said. *I have to live with the consequences.*

I was such an idiot. I'd spent the last few years complaining about all the guys I'd dated—how they were insane libertarians or casual barebackers. And I'd told Vernie that my view of human nature was that people mostly suck. Like I was so much better?

But it was really even worse than that. It was finally hitting me exactly what Kevin and I had done, the reason why I felt like I had concrete of the soul, and why that concrete was hardening even now.

What Kevin and I had had in high school had been something precious, something pure, something wonderful. Yeah, yeah, I'm probably romanticizing our little teenage love all out of proportion, but I'd been romanticizing it all out of proportion for years, so who cares? That's the way I felt about it.

And now I—okay, *we*—had ruined it. We'd trashed it all to hell. Push came to shove, and I'd pushed it into Kevin, and then he'd pushed it into me, even though he was in a monogamous relationship with another guy. The one good thing in my life, the one thing I'd accomplished that I could be truly proud of, and now it was gone.

I guess this was what they meant by a loss of innocence. Who knew?

Kevin sat back down again, even put his arms around me and pulled me close.

"Russel, I'm sorry. That was stupid. We'll figure this out. We *will* be together again, I promise. But you need to give me some time."

Now I stood up from him. I walked toward my clothes and started pulling them on.

"Russel?" Kevin said, but I didn't answer.

Finally I was completely dressed again—even my shoes.

I turned to Kevin. "This *was* a mistake," I said. "And I'm really sorry for my part in it. Don't worry, I'll never tell Colin. But you need to decide what you want—him or me. If you choose me, that's great. I'm totally open to it. And if you choose him, well, I guess that's okay too. You don't owe me anything. But until you decide, I don't think we should see each other, or text, or anything. Especially no sex. And I really mean that this time. I'm unfriending you right now." I did it while he watched. "I mean it. No contact at all. Do you promise?"

He nodded. I could still see his face clearly, and I knew he knew I was right.

And I walked off into the night feeling a little better, thinking, *Okay, so maybe I'm not a complete asshole after all.*

I didn't make it back to the houseboat until after I got home from work the next evening. But I was actually excited to see Min and Gunnar, to tell them everything that had happened. Yes, I'd screwed up, but I'd finally managed to do the right thing in the end, and I was even sort of proud of myself. (I also wanted to tell Min and Gunnar so they could keep me accountable. I was determined that Kevin and I would *not* be hooking up again, no matter how horny or desperate I got. Because clearly he had a meth-like hold over me.)

"Min?" I called around the houseboat. "Gunnar?"

There was music coming from Min's bedroom—soft, low, bluesy. Etta James, I think.

"*You went and said the words,*" the song went. "*Everything was fine before. Then you went and said the words. And now nothin', no nothin', will ever be fine again.*"

I thought, *This ain't good.*

"Min?" I said, approaching the door to her bedroom. It was closed, so I knocked.

"Yeah?" came the voice from inside. It was the softest I think I'd ever heard Min speak.

I opened the door.

Min was lying on her futon in an awkward fetal-esque position even as the singer kept crooning from the iPod.

"*We could say you didn't say 'em. We could say it didn't happen. But you went and said the words. And now I can't, no, you know I can't pretend.*"

"Everything okay?" I said to Min. I knew it wasn't, but I wanted her to be the one to tell me.

She rolled over toward me, and I saw the red in her eyes. Min had been crying. *Min.*

"What happened?" I said.

"It's funny," she said. "The thing they never tell you about polyamory? When you get dumped, you get dumped by two people. And so it feels twice as bad."

And right then I knew that I wasn't going to be telling Min about everything that had happened with Kevin, at least not yet. There was something more important, something she needed to talk about first.

Min's bedroom didn't have room for two people, but I didn't care. I stepped inside anyway, and crawled onto the bed with her. I didn't hug her, because Min's not a hugger (and neither am I). But I lay down on my side next to her, facing her, giving her my full attention and then some.

"Tell me everything that happened," I said.

And so she did.

In the last couple of weeks, Min had felt that Trai and Lena were drifting away from her and closer to each other. But when she'd mentioned it to them, they'd said she was being crazy.

"I lied when I told you before we didn't get jealous," Min told me. "But I just thought it was me being insecure. You know? Feeling like I was the odd one out when I really wasn't, and then actually making it happen by being all clingy? Then last night, they told me they were both busy, that we couldn't get together, which was fine, I didn't really think anything of it. But I woke up in the middle of the night, and I had a flash of jealousy, so I looked them up on the Find My Friends app. And sure enough, they were together. They hadn't even had the decency to block themselves! It's like they wanted me to find out."

Maybe they did, I thought.

"So of course I drove over there," Min said, "and confronted them and made a big scene, and they said they'd been wanting to tell me for a while, but didn't want to hurt me, blah, blah, blah. Everything out of their mouths was such a series of stupid clichés."

I remembered when I'd seen Trai and Lena together out in the parking lot, the night of the Fourth of July. Min had thought they were hiding their physical affection from me. But they'd also been hiding it from her.

"I don't even think Trai's really polyamorous," Min said. "I think it's just an excuse to fuck lots of different people."

It was all I could do not to agree with her. But I'd been around long enough to know that just because people break up, that doesn't mean they might not be back together in a day or a week.

Besides, this was about what Min felt, not me. (See? I'm really *not* an asshole.)

Min and I talked a while a longer. I even got her out of her bedroom and into the living room (it was like coaxing a wet kitten out from under the porch). Once there, I made us both some Top Ramen, and I could tell she hadn't eaten all day since Min normally wouldn't be caught dead eating Top Ramen.

Before I knew it, it was after eleven, and I realized that Gunnar still hadn't come home. When he went home to visit his parents, he was usually back by mid-afternoon.

"Where do you think Gunnar is?" I asked Min.

"I don't know," Min said. "But I was gone for a while. He could've come home and left again."

It was possible that he'd come home and left again. It was also possible that he hadn't made it home at all—that he'd gotten distracted by something somewhere between our hometown and home.

Gunnar had been acting weird enough lately that I wanted to know exactly what was up. But when I texted him, he didn't respond. When I called, he didn't pick up—it went right to voicemail. And unlike Trai and Lena, he'd either blocked himself on Find My Friends, or his phone was off or out of range.

I decided to call his parents. His mom told me that Gunnar had left their house in the early afternoon, just like I'd thought. I didn't want them to worry or to get Gunnar in trouble, so I lied and told them everything was okay, that I thought I heard him coming in the front door just then.

After I ended the call, I looked at Min. This was officially weird. But we still decided not to call the police or anything. After all, Gunnar *was* an adult (of sorts).

We finally went to bed, but in the middle of the night, Min woke me up, concerned. She showed me that Gunnar's bed hadn't been slept in. He hadn't come home that night at all.

CHAPTER FOURTEEN

I was now officially worried about Gunnar.

"We need to do something," Min said. Her eyes were still red—I think the reason she'd checked in on him was because she'd never really gone to sleep herself.

It was almost four in the morning, but we tried texting and calling Gunnar again. He still didn't pick up. Hopefully, his cellphone was just off for the night.

So did we call the police now? I'd heard somewhere that you weren't supposed to contact them until a person had been missing for twenty-four hours, but I had a feeling that was just something they said on TV. Even so, I felt weird about calling them. Gunnar was still an adult (of sorts). And the last thing in the world I wanted to do was upset his parents.

The first thing Min and I did was look for some evidence in the houseboat of where Gunnar might be. He hadn't dated anyone in over a year, and I'd never known him to have anything approaching a one-night stand, but anything was possible (men are pigs). Or maybe he really had come home the day before, in between Min's leaving and coming back again, and maybe he'd left some clue as to where he'd gone after that.

But if Gunnar had left a clue, we couldn't find it. He'd definitely thrown away the Trader Joe's chicken burrito wrapper in the kitchen trash, but I didn't know if he'd done it Sunday or Saturday before we left. Meanwhile, his computer was password protected (and I can barely remember all my *own* passwords, much less his passwords too).

Gunnar's bedroom was on the lower level, and as I was walking back up to the front room, I passed the houseboat's one storage closet. On a lark, I opened it. And yeah, once again, I had to take everything out in order to see the things in the back. But then I realized:

Gunnar's tent is gone. And so is his sleeping bag.

I was instantly relieved. He *had* come home the day before, but then he'd left again, on another Bigfoot search. Of course he had. It! Was! So! Obvious! Why hadn't that occurred to me before?

The point was, everything was okay.

All that said, it did seem odd that he hadn't told Min or me where he was going (or his parents, for that matter). He hadn't even left a note. So something still nagged at me.

I told Min what I'd deduced, and then I went to my computer and started searching for Bigfoot websites. I didn't even know Ben's last name, but it didn't take long to track down his email address (thank you, Bigfoot blimp Kickstarter campaign). Maybe Ben had cellphone coverage even though Gunnar didn't, so I decided to send him an email:

Hey Ben: Hope you guys have finally bagged your Bigfoot. Would you tell Gunnar to call or text me when he gets a chance? He left without telling us where he is. Russel (Gunnar's friend)

By that time, it was still early in the morning, so Min and I both went back to bed.

When we woke up again, I had to go to work (at Bake) and Min had a seminar.

It was just after noon when I finally heard back from Ben:

Gunnar's not with me. We may have a problem. Call me ASAP.

I was instantly worried again. I took a break as soon as possible and called Ben (he'd sent me his number).

"There was another Bigfoot sighting, on Saturday," he told me. "A good one too—Class A. These are the ones you really pay attention to, sort of like a close encounter of the third kind."

Ah HA! I thought, even though this totally wasn't the time.

"So is that where you are?" I said. "Did Gunnar leave early or something?"

"We didn't go. It was too remote. Private property, and the only access is logging roads." What had Ben said before about loggers? Something about how they see Bigfoot in the distant backcountry?

"But Gunnar's tent and sleeping bag are missing," I said.

"That's exactly what I was afraid of. We were all discussing the sighting on Saturday night, online. Gunnar had really wanted to check it out—he'd argued that we should do it. *Strenuously.* But it was too hard to get to. This is exactly the kind of thing the Bigfoot blimp would be perfect for."

Enough with the stupid blimp! I thought. *Where's Gunnar?*

"In the end, I thought Gunnar agreed with us," Ben said. "I wish the coordinates hadn't been listed on our website. I had no idea he'd go on his own."

Ordinarily I wouldn't think that Gunnar would be stupid enough to do something like this on his own either. As strange as he could be, he never took risks. But it had been weeks since he'd been acting normal. Something was going on with him, and it had something to do with this damn Bigfoot obsession.

"Well, he's not in any real danger," I said, forcing a laugh. "Right? I mean, it's not like anything bad is going to happen."

Ben didn't say anything for a second.

"Ben?" I said.

"I won't lie to you. Those logging roads can be pretty screwed up. It's way too easy to get lost and run out of gas. And who knows if there's even a trail?" He hesitated a second, then he said, "It also doesn't help that he's gone deep into grizzly country."

As Min had recently pointed out, I'm a terrible liar, so I went back inside Bake and told Jake and Amanda the truth about what was going on. I was hoping they'd be all concerned and offer to let me leave early for the day, but they didn't. When I asked outright, Jake said, "Sorry, we really need you today."

Later, we got a nasty complaint from a customer, and after the customer left, Jake turned to Amanda and said, "That was *your* fault."

"How do you know I burned the loaf?" Amanda said. "Maybe *you* baked it." That's when I knew for a fact Amanda had baked it. If she hadn't, she would've blamed it on me.

"That was a gluten-free loaf," Jake lectured. "Gluten-free has to be baked at a lower temperature than the others."

"Seriously?" she said. "You're seriously telling me this? The person whose idea it was to have gluten-free bread in the first place?"

I simultaneously rolled my eyes and shook my head. If Jake and Amanda had to argue about every little thing, couldn't they at least argue about letting me go home early?

By the time I got home that night, it was after eight p.m. Min was home too. It was too late to leave for the woods, but Ben and Katie lived in Cle Elum, this little town in the middle of the Cascade Mountains. It was a couple of hours closer to where Gunnar supposedly was, so Ben said we could come and spend the night with them. Min and I threw some things together and left right away. Min drove, and on the way I worked my usual magic, swapping work schedules via text in order to get the next day off.

It was almost midnight by the time we arrived at Ben and Katie's. They lived in a small cedar cabin on the outskirts of town. Ben invited us inside to the front room. They had lots of bookshelves with what looked to be just about every book ever written about Bigfoot.

As for Katie, I'm not saying she was any less committed to the search for Bigfoot than Ben, but in the hours since Min and I had left Seattle, she'd made us an impressive-looking batch of Rice Krispies treats (with mini M&Ms).

"Tell me about this latest sighting," I said to them, later, over hot tea and treats. "What made Gunnar so excited to go there?"

"It was a compelling one, that's for sure," Ben said. "It was a group of loggers—five in all—and best of all, a forester, someone with actual scientific background. One of them noticed a figure watching them from the top of a nearby ridge. His first thought was, 'A gorilla has escaped the zoo.' But of course that made no sense at all, not where they were. He pointed it out to the others. They all saw it. And they took photos."

Ben nodded down to blown-up photographs right in front of me on the coffee table. I wasn't sure how I'd missed them before.

Like every Bigfoot photo ever taken, it was impossible to know anything for sure. None of the pictures were completely clear, and they'd been taken from pretty far away. But whatever the thing was, it definitely looked to be walking across this rocky ridge—*walking*, not crawling. In other words, it was definitely no grizzly bear.

"Those loggers were out in the middle of nowhere," Ben said. "If this was a prank, it was a pretty damn elaborate one."

As interesting as this was, I was more concerned about Gunnar. "So just how dangerous is this place we're going?" I asked.

Katie nodded down to the photos. "Dangerous enough that we saw *these*, and decided not to go there."

"Honestly, I'm mostly worried about Gunnar getting lost," Ben said.

"What about the grizzlies?" I said.

He smiled. "It's not like in the movies. Bears try hard to avoid people—even grizzlies." He looked at Min. "But it is true they're attracted to women menstruating."

"That's not a problem," Min said.

"But it's not just the area that has me worried," Ben said. "It's Gunnar. The way he's been acting. At first, it was great having someone younger get so excited about Bigfoot. But then I met him in person, on that trip. And ever since then...well, to tell you the truth, he's sort of scared me. Even if we had decided to do this expedition, I wouldn't have invited him. I gather he hasn't always been so intense?"

"No," I said. "This is something new. And we've been just as baffled by it as you."

But later that night in the bedroom Min and I shared (our idea), I said to her, "I feel guilty. It's obvious that something's been going on with Gunnar. I mean, Ben barely knows Gunnar, and he picked up on it right away. But I've been so caught up in my own life that I just sort of ignored it."

"Me too," she said.

The lights were off, and we laid in the darkness for a few minutes.

"Gunnar's going to be okay, right?" Min said.

"Yeah," I said, sounding so certain that I almost believed it myself.

We left early the next morning in a two-car caravan with Clive and Leon. Min and I rode in the car with Ben and Katie.

Once we were on the road, I said, "Maybe we should call the ranger station."

"And say what?" Ben said. "That someone went on a hike? Besides, where he went, it's not exactly legal. He could get arrested. Let's see if we can find him on our own first."

We drove for a long time. Along the way, I kept checking my messages and trying to contact Gunnar. But I quickly lost my coverage, and I never got it back.

We kept driving north along a two-lane highway.

Then we left the highway and turned onto a side road. We were traveling northwest now, and going up, deep into the North Cascade Mountains.

Eventually our paved road became a gravel road. The smell of dust was even stronger than the pine and fir trees that surrounded us.

Finally, we came to another gravel road, this one blocked by a metal gate.

We got out and inspected it. It wasn't locked, but there was a place for a padlock, and the metal was dented. Someone had broken the lock, maybe with a rock. It had to be Gunnar, but I'd never known him to break a law in his life. This wasn't like him at all.

I'd thought the gravel road we were on was as bad as the roads were going to get. What I didn't know was that logging roads, at least the logging roads be-hind locked metal gates, are barely even roads. They're more like "suggested guidelines" for your ve-hicle. I guess when you're in a harvester or a loader (different kinds of logging tractors), things like "an actual road" just aren't that important.

But Ben and the others had four-wheel drive, so for the time being, we were okay.

We wound our way through the logging roads for a long time. I read once that the difference between a "labyrinth" and a "maze" is that a labyrinth has only one path that winds like crazy to the end, whereas a maze has an endless number of off-shoots and dead-ends before you finally reach your destination.

I don't think these roads were either a labyrinth *or* a maze, because it didn't seem like they were leading anywhere at all.

Ben had GPS which he used to follow the coordi-nates of the loggers. But the area was hilly, and some of it had been clear-cut already, but most of it had not. All this interfered with the GPS. Needless to say, there weren't any signs or numbered markings on the trees. And even if we found the right spot, what guarantee did we have that Gunnar had found it too? The thing we were most worried about was Gunnar getting lost. But how did you find someone who was lost—someone who himself didn't even know where he was?

And no, this time, that's not a metaphor for my own life. It was Gunnar I was worried about at this point, not me.

Then, totally without warning, we came to Gun-nar's car, parked alongside the "road."

I exhaled for what seemed like the first time in five hours.

It had been so long since I'd seen any color other than shades of green or brown that it was a little shocking to see Gunnar's red Geo Prizm. I don't know how that little car had made it this far in, but it had me worried about Gunnar's sanity all over again.

We climbed out of our car and looked around.

Ben referred to his GPS device. "The ridge is that way," he said, pointing.

Now I saw why Gunnar had stopped where he did. The "road" continued forward, but Ben was pointing into a massive, fresh clear-cut. It just wasn't passable by any vehicle that didn't have tank treads.

I was about to suggest honking the horn, trying to get Gunnar's attention. But then I heard the roar of distant chainsaws coming from farther down the main road. We couldn't take the chance of those loggers hearing us too.

Following Ben's GPS device, the six of us headed off into that clear-cut on foot.

There were pine needles *everywhere*, a layer of green snow that made the ground feel both slippery and springy. All around us, massive tree stumps loomed, chopped and twisted, their gnarled roots reaching out in front of us. The trees themselves were all gone, but most of their branches had been stripped and piled into giant heaps—like funeral pyres waiting to be lit. It all made for such an alien landscape, a cross between total desolation and something stark and beautiful.

This had been an older forest—it was the only way to explain the size of those trunks. That made the land seem even more sacred, the clear-cut even more profane. The ground had been raped, which is probably insensitive to say, but that's how it felt—like it was lying there naked, exposed. It was almost embarrassing, the way we could see every contour, every hill rising and falling. And because the land was so irregular, it was impossible to see very far head. It was also interfering with the GPS device again.

But Ben's compass still worked, so forward we hiked. The twigs and needles crunched under our feet—at least I'd remembered to wear boots this time. The stench of pitch was overwhelming, so strong it was giving me a headache.

We'd been hiking for at least half an hour when I felt a tickle in my nose. I knew that feeling well.

Another bloody nose, I thought.

At first I didn't think much more about it. It was annoying, but like I said before, I got lots of nosebleeds—I always had. And, as always, I'd brought Kleenex.

Then I remembered what Ben had said about bears being attracted to menstruating women.

Ben looked back at me, saw the bloody Kleenex in my hand. We'd already been hiking a while, so it's not like I could go back to the car, especially not by myself. Besides, what about Gunnar?

"It's fine," Ben said, but a moment or two later, a gust of wind blew, reminding me that the scent of my blood was now being carried far and wide.

Onward we walked. Then the land dipped down and we rounded a bend, and suddenly, somehow, we were surrounded by trees—actual trees, not hacked-off stumps.

"It must be a wetland," Ben said. "A pond or a lake. The loggers are required by law to keep a buffer around water."

It was definitely an older forest, a tiny fragment of the kind of woods that had once covered the entire area. Ben consulted his compass again, then nodded us forward, deeper into the trees.

The land was dressed again at last, and it was all graceful, flowing clothing—sweeping boughs and ruffled ferns. The hemlocks were like lace, and the moss dripped down like stoles. The smells were different here, more complicated, richer, but softer. Everything was soothing, even the sounds, and I couldn't remember when we'd stopped hearing the distant buzz of chain saws.

Ben was right: it was a swamp. Silver pools appeared on our left, languid and still, winding between the tree trunks. But unlike the one by the stinky picnic gazebo, this swamp smelled clean.

I remembered what Ben had said before, the first time I met him, about those Bigfoot eyewitnesses having the sense they were being watched. Suddenly I had that sense too. Or did I? Had I remembered what Ben had said and was now just imagining things?

We trudged on through the trees. The ground was wet here, even muddy in places, but there were no footprints, no sign that Gunnar had come this way before us.

But we weren't alone either. As we walked forward through that ancient forest, a great hairy beast lumbered into view in front of us, not twenty feet away— and this was definitely no grizzly bear.

CHAPTER FIFTEEN

It wasn't Bigfoot either. It was a moose. Sorry about that. It just seemed like things needed a little livening up there.

But there really was a moose. And the thing is, moose aren't anything to sneeze at, especially bull moose, which this one was. It had ridiculously skinny legs, but a massive body and an incredible rack of antlers on its head. The tips were sharp, reaching out in opposite directions like the two sides of a surprisingly scary Rorschach test (one I was failing).

The moose snorted, bobbing its head. Then it stared out at us from under that rack of sharp antlers.

The blood rushed from my nose in a sudden surge. It hadn't ever occurred to me that my nose would bleed faster during times of stress—and this was definitely a time of stress. But it made total sense. My heart was pumping something crazy.

"It's okay," Ben said quietly, gently. "Everything will be fine just as long as we don't make any sudden moves."

We started backing away. The moose huffed and shuffled its feet. Its hide was black and shaggy. And unlike the rest of this forest, it didn't smell soft and complicated—it just stank. We could smell it from twenty feet away.

Fortunately, the moose was already bored with us. It shambled off into the swamp.

I dabbed my nose. I'd brought Kleenex, but only three pieces, and now they were all completely soaked through with blood. I'd basically unfurled a blood-soaked flag and was now waving it at all the grizzlies.

We hurried onward through the woods, past the silver water, and the ground started rising again, sharply. Despite the strenuousness of the uphill climb, my bloody nose stopped at last. Up ahead, the trees fell away again, opening out into another clear-cut. Beyond that was a rocky ridge that definitely could have been the one that Ben had shown me in the photos.

There was another flash of unusual color nestled in with all those stumps and branches. It was blue this time.

Gunnar's tent. It had to be. We'd found him. But was he okay?

I started toward the tent, ahead of the others. "Gunnar?" I called.

But I was too enthusiastic—or maybe I was still a little wobbly from seeing the moose (and losing all that blood).

I stumbled backward, out of the clear-cut, back into the trees and undergrowth.

My arms flailed.

Then I fell.

I was sliding down, back toward the swamp and the moose. It wasn't a cliff or anything—it was more of a long, sharp slope. At least I somehow managed to twist myself around, forward, so I was sliding down on my butt. But I was still hitting every rock and root. I tore at the loam, which was dark and rich. I could hear ferns ripping all around me as I flew through them.

Toward the bottom of the hill, I finally stopped. At least I hadn't gone into the swamp. But the world spun around me. Everything smelled of pine and dirt and torn foliage. I had something nasty in my mouth—not dirt, I realized, but yellow spores from the underside of the ferns.

I looked down at the front of my shirt. It was covered with blood.

I'm dying! I thought. I'd been impaled by a sharp pine branch, or maybe the antlers of that moose.

I glanced around, hyperventilating, but I didn't see a branch or the moose. Even so, I could feel my lifeblood leaching away with every beat of my heart. I only had seconds left to live.

No, wait, I thought. *I just have a bloody nose again.* I must have hit my nose during the fall, and it had started back up. So I was fine. But man, I had lost a lot of blood. It really did smell metallic, like copper.

"Russel!" Min called from above. "Are you okay?"

"Yeah," I said. "I'm fine." I felt like an idiot that I'd just lost my balance and fallen backward off the hill. At least I'd realized I wasn't dying before I'd started screaming my head off. That *really* would've been embarrassing.

The sight and smell of all that blood was actually sort of disturbing, so I held my nose until it stopped again. That's when I also realized that I was covered with some pretty nasty scrapes. I struggled upright. The aches wound around my body in streaks, almost like a tiger's stripes.

By now the others had worked their way down the hillside toward me—more slowly, careful not to lose their balance too.

I saw Min first, then Ben. They both looked really concerned.

"I just had another bloody nose," I said, explaining all the blood.

Clive and Katie and Leon stepped into view behind Min and Ben.

And then came Gunnar behind them, looking just as concerned as the others, not crazed at all. He must have joined them up at the top of the hillside.

"You're okay!" I said.

"Of course I'm okay," he said, like the whole idea of his not being okay just confused him. "But ooohh, boy, do you look like shit."

Min and Gunnar and Ben and the others fussed over me for a few minutes (something I secretly enjoyed). I also appreciated that no one made me feel like an idiot. I completely deserved it, but still.

Finally, Gunnar said to all of us, "What are you guys *doing* here?"

Both Min and I just glared at him, as if to say, "*REALLY?*"

"Okay, yeah," he admitted. "Coming here was stupid. You tracked me down, huh? But I really needed to do this."

I looked over at Ben and the others. "Give us a minute?" I felt bad asking them to leave, after everything they'd done for us—for Gunnar. But there were things I needed to say to Gunnar, and things I hoped he would finally explain to me, and I had a feeling it could get personal.

Once the others had walked away, I said to Gunnar, "What's really going on? Why'd you come all the way out here by yourself?"

He sat back into the ferns, crushing them. "I don't know. It's all been so strange since my dad got cancer."

Min and I looked at each other, and then we both sank down into the foliage in front of Gunnar.

"Your dad has *cancer*?" Min said. "Why didn't you *say* anything?" No doubt this was why Gunnar hadn't wanted me to come inside his parents' house that day—he hadn't wanted me to know.

Gunnar tried to find the words. "I guess I thought if I didn't think about it, if I didn't say it out loud to you guys, it wouldn't be real."

"Is he going to be okay?" I said.

"No," Gunnar said. "It's bad. Liver cancer. Months to live and all that."

Part of me was thinking, *Then what the hell are you doing lost in these woods, totally out of contact, you idiot?!* But I had a feeling that Gunnar's family knew him well enough to know that he could be pretty unpredictable.

That's when something else occurred to me: was this what Gunnar's Bigfoot obsession was about— what it had *always* been about?

I thought back to the night Gunnar had first told us about Bigfoot. We'd thought he had something really important to tell us. Instead, he'd told us the origin of the word "Sasquatch."

That's the night he found out about his dad, I thought. And it's why he'd been especially weird since then.

And why the hell not? If your dad has incurable cancer, there's not really anything you can do. It's either going to kill him, or it isn't, and you're completely powerless. But not so with the search for Bigfoot. With Bigfoot, you can interview eyewitnesses, make plaster casts of footprints, take expeditions deeper and deeper into the woods, even build a goddamn Bigfoot blimp. When it comes to Bigfoot, there's *always* something more you can do. And the best part is that Bigfoot isn't real, so you can search forever, and you never have to give up hope. Bigfoot is always waiting around the next river bend, or hiding inside the trees one forest over.

The whole idea of searching for Bigfoot because your dad is dying of cancer suddenly seemed so touching and awesome that I felt myself wanting to cry (or maybe it was all the aches and scrapes, especially one scratch on my right calf that *really* stung).

And then I had a really interesting thought. Maybe this was what *all* of Gunnar's weird obsessions were about—what they'd *always* been about. Rather than deal with something unpleasant in his life, he channeled his feelings and anxiety into something entirely different—something more or less manageable and understandable. I couldn't help but think: *Is there any way that strategy might work for me?* Then again, I guess I already had plenty of illusions of my own to cling to—plenty of paper lanterns to cover those harsh, bare light bulbs.

"I feel like an idiot," I said.

"Come on," Min said. "So you fell down a hill."

I laughed. "That's actually not what I was talking about. And it's incredibly sad that I have *two* things to be embarrassed about right now."

"What else are you embarrassed about?" Gunnar said to me.

"I've been jealous of you both."

"Jealous?" Min said. "Of us?"

Then I remembered what Vernie sometimes (jokingly) said: *Enough about you, let's talk about me!* Gunnar had just told us his dad was dying of cancer, but I was making it all about me.

"Nothing," I said. "Never mind."

"Russ?" Gunnar said. "Come on. Talk to us."

So I explained how I'd started to think of them—of everyone around me—as having either Unstoppable Career Drive or Passionate Aimlessness, but I didn't have either.

"That's crazy," Min said.

"How is it crazy?" I said. "You're twenty-three years old, and you've already got your whole life mapped out. Not to mention the fact that you also totally understand the whole physical universe."

Min laughed out loud, but not at me. It was such a bawdy, open-throated laugh that I somehow instantly knew she was laughing at herself.

"Russel," she said, her face softening. "I'm in *grad school*. Don't you know the whole point of grad school? It's so you don't have to make any actual decisions. I don't know what I want to do with my whole *life*. I like physics, so I picked it. But I don't know if it's what I want to 'do'. I have no idea. And you're forgetting something about my life—namely, the fact that I've just spent the last three months trying to figure out if I wanted to try a relationship with Trai and Lena, if I might be poly, only to finally say yes, and then have them turn around and dump me three weeks later."

Gunnar hadn't heard this part yet, so Min turned to him, as if to explain. But he cut her off with a nod.

"You're polyamorous," he said. "I know."

Typical Gunnar, I thought. He had a way of always understanding more than you thought.

"And look at *me*," Gunnar said to me. "I'm so screwed up that I can't deal with the fact that my dad's dying. Instead, I have to go on a hunt for Bigfoot. And you think *you're* the idiot?"

I smiled. So Gunnar knew exactly what he'd been doing all summer, that it had been a conscious strategy. Somehow that figured too.

"Face it, Russel," Min said. "We're all just faking it. Gunnar, me, probably everyone. You're not any different from anyone else. Some of us are just better at hiding it."

I didn't say anything, just looked back and forth between my friends, the three of us sitting in that tangle of torn-up ferns (and a virtual puddle of my own blood).

Nobody knows anything. That's what Vernie had said, but it wasn't only a famous quote by some screenwriter talking about Hollywood. Nobody knows anything about anything. I'd thought it was just me, but it wasn't. *Nobody* really knows what life is about. We're all just trying to make sense of something that doesn't make much sense.

Was this the secret to life—the thing I'd figured everyone knew except me? It was so obvious! And yet, it kind of wasn't. It was something I hadn't even known I didn't know. How *would* I know that every-one else was feeling this too if they're doing such a good job of hiding it? How would *anyone* know?

That's when something else hit me. Maybe nobody knows anything, but I did know one thing for sure: how important my friends were. They were the one and only reason I'd survived my teen years. And they were probably going to be the only reason I'd survive my twenties too.

I know a lot of people say their husband or their wife is the most important person in their life. I didn't have a husband, and given how I kept screwing it up with Kevin, I probably never would. But even if I did, and if we had kids one day, I wondered if they'd be more important to me than Min and Gunnar. As important? Sure. But *more* important? It was hard to imagine being closer to anyone than I felt to Gunnar and Min right then. And that made me wonder if somehow the very state of being gay, or maybe just being different and bullied and picked on, had some-how made my friendships more real, more important, more close. And *that* made me remember what Vernie had said about discrimination making gay people more interesting. Were these sorts of friendships the kind of thing LGBT people would be losing in ten or twenty years, once anti-gay discrimination was gone completely? Would it be worth it? Vernie had said suffering was always pointless, and I'd agreed then, and I still agreed. But I couldn't help but wonder.

Anyway, maybe this, learning how truly great my friends were, was the real thing I didn't know I didn't know. Except I *had* known. I'd just forgotten for a while.

"I don't know what I'd do without you guys," I said, putting my arms around them both. "But the next time we have to admit something real and important to each other, let's do it over cocktails on top of the houseboat, okay? Let's not have to come all the way out into these freakin' woods."

Min laughed too, but Gunnar didn't, not even a little.

"What?" I said, looking at him.

"I dunno. I'm really glad I came out here."

"You are? Why?"

"Oh, that's right, I didn't get a chance to tell you. I saw Bigfoot."

Min turned to stare at him now too. But he just kept looking back at us, with no impishness on his mouth or in his eyes—not a trace.

"Gunnar," Min said. "This is a serious moment. Come on, be serious."

"I *am* serious. It was this morning. I got out of my tent, and the world was completely still. And it was like Ben up at Stehekin. I turned around, and there he was, fifteen feet away. It was Bigfoot. Eight feet tall, covered with hair, definitely intelligent—not human, but definitely more human than ape. He was real, and he was right in front of me."

I honestly didn't know what to say. Finally, I said, "Did you take a photo?"

"I thought about it," Gunnar said. "But I decided not to. If you'd asked before if I'd take a photo, I'd have said, 'Heck, yeah!' But seeing him, I thought, 'Why?' The people who believe already believe, and the people who don't never will. Besides, there just seemed something wrong about it. Bigfoot are hiding for a reason. And this one was showing himself to me for a reason too. I'm still not sure what those reasons are, so for the time being, I decided it was best to let them go on hiding."

Min didn't say anything, just kept staring at him. I wasn't sure which of their two faces was more interesting: Gunnar's look of complete innocence, or Min's expression of a wonder that was just as pure.

As for me, part of me thought Gunnar couldn't possibly have been serious, that he had to be playing a prank on Min and me. But later, he repeated the same story to Ben and the others, and he sounded absolutely sincere.

To this day, I still have no idea whether Gunnar was telling the truth. But I do know that Min believes him, and to my mind, that's almost as interesting.

It was dark by the time we got home that night.

Min, Gunnar, and I walked down the dock toward the houseboat. The boards creaked, but the lake was still. The water smelled like rain—clean but full of flavor.

And there, waiting in the shadows of the porch to our house was a figure—a guy. I couldn't see his face—Min and I had forgotten to leave the porch light on when we'd left.

You need to decide what you want—him or me, I'd said to Kevin. *But until you decide, I don't think we should see each other.*

So had he decided? Was it really me he wanted?

THE THING I DIDN'T KNOW I DIDN'T KNOW

CHAPTER SIXTEEN

Another shadowy figure stepped up next to the first one, then both of them walked forward into the light from another porch. They were both small and wearing dark earth tones.

In other words, it wasn't Kevin waiting for me to come home—it was Trai and Lena waiting for Min. (Now that I knew the reason they'd been acting so weird around me, I couldn't call them "Min-ions" anymore, could I?)

Min froze. She stared at them. And they looked back at her.

Trai and Lena both smiled. They had that frazzled, open-faced look that a lover has when he or she—or *they*—come to your house in the middle of the night to apologize. It was the expression I'd been hoping to see on Kevin's face. They wanted her back.

I wanted to be happy for her—I *was* happy for her. But still. My heart dropped like an anchor in a bottomless ocean. How could I have mistaken Trai for Kevin in the first place? They didn't look *anything* alike. I guess I'd just wanted it so bad.

Min didn't run toward them. Instead, she turned to Gunnar and me.

Gunnar hadn't been involved in the whole polyamorous thing. But I had. And I nodded to Min. "Go," I said. It didn't take away anything from Gunnar and me that her boyfriend and girlfriend had come back.

At first, I'd had a hard time understanding why anyone would want to be in a polyamorous relationship. It would be so complicated being with two other people. But now I saw that I'd *been* in a relationship with two other people—Min and Gunnar—and it was the best, most rewarding relationship of my life. I had no interest in being romantic with either of them (the understatement of the century!). But what if someone else did? It made more sense to me now.

Min walked toward Lena and Trai, and they walked toward her. They met on the dock in the dark.

Gunnar and I went into the houseboat, giving Min and Trai and Lena their privacy. Gunnar was exhausted and immediately went to bed. But I wasn't. The wheels in my brain were spinning. I couldn't have slept if I'd tried.

Instead, I sat down at my computer and started writing. It wasn't the story of my life—it was completely different. It was a fantasy story about a guy lost in an enchanted forest. He didn't know how he'd gotten there or where he was going, and the trail was so bad that he kept losing it, only to find himself in the middle of different adventures. He met a wise old mentor and he vanquished an evil knight, and I had a feeling there'd be a warring king and queen somewhere along the way.

I wasn't exactly sure where the story was going.

But the weird thing was, the feelings of the main character were actually very familiar. The guy kept losing the trail (sometimes he was led astray), but somehow he always made his way back. He didn't know where the trail was leading, but it had to be leading somewhere, and he was determined to see it through, to get to the end.

I knew this guy, because I was this guy.

Anyway, I wrote for hours and hours. And I know I shouldn't have been surprised by this, not in the least, but I totally was: the story came out in the form of a screenplay.

"So I think I know what I want to do with my life," I said to Vernie, a week or so later, after I invited myself over to her house for tea. We were sitting at her dining room table.

"You *do*?" Vernie said, nibbling on one of the tiny sandwiches she'd insisted on making.

"Don't laugh. I think I want to try being a screenwriter."

"Why would I laugh?"

"Because I bet people have come up to you all your life and said they want to be screenwriters—not really thinking that it's a whole, like, craft that you've spent your life mastering."

"Sure, they have. But so what? There was a time when I said, 'I think I wanna try being a screenwriter.' Thank God people didn't laugh at me. Come to think of it, they *did* laugh. Everyone I knew. But thank God I didn't listen." She sipped her tea. "What made you realize it?"

"It was something you said. You said that every life is cinematic—you just need to know when to fade to black. Ever since you said it, it's made more and more sense."

"That did it, huh?"

"Yeah. Why?"

"I thought it might have been when I invited you over to dinner to dazzle you with all my writer friends. Or that time we went to a movie, so I could give you my patented lecture on what makes a good story."

"Wait," I said. "Go back. You knew?"

"That you're a born writer? Of course I knew. The first time we met, you quoted Tennessee Williams."

"I thought that was a gay thing."

"It's a gay thing *and* a writer thing. Let's face it: there's a lot of overlap. That's why I like gay guys. Everything you do is so much larger than life. Yes, yes, that's a hoary stereotype, and there are plenty of boring gay guys these days, guys who are determined to be exactly like everyone else. I'm old school— humor me, okay? Anyway, movies are larger than life too. That's why they're so much *better* than life. Don't you see? *You're* larger than life."

Me? I thought. In my entire life, no one had ever accused me of being larger than life (melodramatic, yes—larger than life, no). On the other hand, I also hadn't thought of my life as particularly cinematic. But thanks to Vernie, I now saw that it sort of was— at least if you arranged things in a certain way.

"It's not the way you act," Vernie said, somehow reading the thoughts on my face. "It's the way you *think*. You think like a storyteller. Just like I do.

Which, for the record, means I wasn't very subtle when I tried to get you into screenwriting."

"Or setting me up with Felicks."

She cackled.

"But I think I know what you mean," I said. "Writers try to make sense out of life. Is that right? They divide it up and give it structure. They find the beginning and the end. Then they try to give it all a point, make it feel like it's going somewhere. It's like the day I saved you from drowning. That was the beginning of our story together."

"And this conversation is the end?"

"Oh, God, I hope not!"

"Well, I hope you know that at some point, you're going to have to move to Los Angeles."

"Really? Why?"

"It's partly about connections. More than anything—*much* more than actual talent—making movies is about who you know. And the best way to meet someone important is to meet them *before* they're important. Like, they're doing their laundry next to you at the laundromat. Then, two months later, they have a three-picture deal. After that, who knows? Maybe they'll even still take your call. But it's not just the connections. It's also something about the vibe of the city. There's something in the air. All the crazy dreamers move to Los Angeles."

"You don't live there," I said.

"Yes, well, all those crazy dreamers also move away again after their dreams are crushed. But that's okay. It makes way for the next generation of crazy dreamers. The circle of life and all that."

"Is it really that bad?"

"It'll completely destroy your soul. On the other hand, how great for your soul are the two jobs you have now?"

Vernie had a way of cutting right through the bullshit, didn't she? But I was definitely intrigued. Could I really move to California?

Vernie slapped the table. "Hold on, that's it! I saved your life! I predicted I would, and I did."

"How exactly did you save my life?"

"I convinced you to go into screenwriting."

"And I appreciate that," I said. "But that didn't 'save' my life. I mean, it's not like I'm going to *die* if I don't become a screenwriter."

"Close enough!"

"No, it's not. You're totally forcing it. If this was a movie, nobody would buy it."

"Oh, please. They would too! It's emotionally right on point."

I shook my head. "Nuh uh."

"What are you, six? I can't believe this! It's completely obvious that I saved your life, and you're denying it."

"Okay, okay," I said, laughing. "You saved my life."

Her face brightened. "Really? My dream was right? And you admit it?"

I held up my hands in total surrender. "I admit it."

"In that case," she said, primly rising from her chair, "you may now have a piece of berry tart."

"No, really," I said, more serious now, stopping her with my hand. "Vernie? You really did save my life. You gave my life meaning, which I now see is just about as important as oxygen. So...thank you."

Vernie stared at me, but only for a second. Then she snatched her arm away. "Oh, stop it! You gay men and your cheap sentiment. Do you have to turn everything into a Lifetime movie?"

But those were just the words she said. What she was feeling was totally different. I know this because even though she turned quickly for the kitchen again, it wasn't fast enough to hide the tears in her eyes.

I'd like to be able to report that my deciding to become a screenwriter finally gave me an Unstoppable Career Drive (and also a bit of Passionate Aimlessness, because, let's face it, screenwriting is a lot more fun than most other jobs).

It didn't, not really. Every now and then writing felt like the night after we found Gunnar in the woods. But most of the time I had to *force* myself to sit down at that computer, and a lot of the time nothing really came out even when I did. And when I did finally finish that screenplay, no one in Hollywood even wanted to read the damn thing. Vernie read it, and she was very encouraging, but she also said, "Screenplays are like pancakes. Sometimes you have to just throw the first one away."

I'd also like to be able to report that discovering that everyone else was mostly faking it in life—that I now knew the thing I didn't know I didn't know before—had made me more connected to the people I live with and the people I share a planet with. But the feeling was fleeting. I was definitely closer to Min and Gunnar, at least until Min left a note accusing me of stealing her muffins, and Gunnar became obsessed with cheese-making—specifically, very stinky cheese-making.

Speaking of Min, she and Trai and Lena didn't get back together after all. They talked about it, but in the end, Min decided it didn't feel right. A few months later, Lena broke up with Trai too, and she and Min dated briefly, but then Min broke that off as well. As for being polyamorous, she told me she was still open to the idea, but that there *was* more drama than in a two-person relationship, and it was too much for her for the time being.

I still hated my job at Green Lake, but things got more relaxed when the summer season ended and I moved back into the indoor swimming pool. But my job at Bake got worse, so I guess it all sort of evened out.

Gunnar's dad died in November, and the funeral was very sad (Gunnar's eulogy was pitch-perfect—funny, touching, and wise).

The point of all this is that my life was sometimes shitty, occasionally awesome, but mostly just sort of okay.

But don't get me wrong. I did feel better than before. Now I had a direction, and that really is a huge deal.

As for Kevin, I didn't call or email or text or even cyber-stalk him. I hadn't been sure I had it in me, but I was really happy to find out that I did.

Then around mid-November, Min and Gunnar and I were home alone one night, all in the front room. Min was studying; Gunnar was browsing YouTube videos, currently between obsessions; and I was playing my brand spanking new copy of *Dragon Age: Inquisition* on the Xbox (totally worth the wait).

And there was a knock on the door. The docks to the houseboats are gated and locked—too many tourists—so it's always kind of surprising when someone comes right to the door. But it could have been a neighbor, or an especially persistent Christian missionary. (It wouldn't have been the first. What, do they climb over the fence?)

I was focused on the game, so Min answered it. Somewhere in the back of my mind, I smelled a swirl of fresh air slipping in from outside. But I was playing my new video game, so, well, fuck that.

"Russel?" Min said. "It's for you."

I paused the game and turned.

Kevin was standing in that open doorway. His hair was shorter than before, and he'd shaved his beard, but mostly what I noticed was that his face was as wide as the open ocean. Honestly, I'd never seen him look so good, which is really saying something because I'd seen him naked.

As great as *Dragon Age* was, it simply didn't exist anymore. I stood up and walked over to Kevin. I felt both Min and Gunnar's eyes on us, burning like laser beams.

"Can we go somewhere to talk?" Kevin said.

"Yeah," I said. "Of course." Part of me wanted to soar up right through the ceiling like Iron Man, screaming, "KEVIN WANTS ME, KEVIN WANTS ME!" But I didn't want to jump to any conclusions—maybe he was here selling magazine subscriptions.

So I grabbed my jacket, and we went for a walk along the lake. It was well after dark—the days had gotten a lot shorter—and the air was cool and wet. It was the time of year in Seattle when everything is so damp that your bath towel never really dries completely, not even twenty-four hours after you've used it.

"So," he said. "I left Colin."

"You *did*?"

He nodded in the dark. "Three weeks ago." He stopped and faced me. "I want to be with you. And I wanted to know if you still want to be with me."

I wasn't even tempted to joke with him, to pretend like I was seeing someone else, or I'd suddenly realized I was straight.

"Yeah," I said. "I still want to be with you."

We kissed right there on the boardwalk.

(For what it's worth, I apologize for making you wait this long to find out if Kevin and I got back together. Then again, I had to wait all the way until the middle of November to find out myself, so you can just deal. As for whether *this* is a fake, feel-good happy ending like in *Pretty Woman*, well, it was definitely feel-good, at least for me. But fake? I don't think so, mostly because I'd like to think I earned it.)

Finally, we turned and started walking again, toward downtown.

"Why?" I said.

"Huh?" Kevin said.

"Why'd you pick me?"

"I can't answer that."

"Sure, you can. It was the night I came for dinner, wasn't it? You realized what a total asshole Colin was?"

"No, I still don't blame him for that. He was just

reacting to me. He sensed something that I didn't want to admit."

"What's that?"

"That I was still in love with you."

I smiled. I guess I'd known this was what he was going to say—it's what Min had said all those months ago. But it was still nice to hear.

"I feel horrible about what I did to him," Kevin said. "I hope that he'll forgive me one day, and he and I can be friends."

This was less nice to hear, since I remembered what had happened the last time Kevin had wanted to be "friends" with an ex-boyfriend. Then I realized how petty I was being. No matter how much of a jerk Colin was, Kevin and I had both treated him like shit, and the fact that we'd acted sort of honorably at the end didn't really change that. Besides, I was the one who'd ended up with Kevin, so the least I could do was be magnanimous.

Kevin and I walked on through the night, and he told me more about the breakup itself—how exactly it had gone down, how ugly it had been. I told him how sorry I was that he'd had to go through all that alone, but we both knew it had probably been better for Colin's sake.

Before I knew it, we found ourselves in Seattle Center, the site of the old world's fair, now this big city park. It's the location of the Space Needle, which was still open, even though it was after eleven p.m.

We bought tickets and took the elevator up to the observation deck. On the ride up, the elevator operator told us that the Space Needle was over five hundred feet tall, which, ironically, was the same height that Vernie and I had been at when we'd had coffee at the Starbucks on the fortieth floor of the Columbia Center (for *free*, except that totally wasn't the point).

Part of the observation deck is outside, an open-air ring all the way around the saucer. It was even colder up there than it had been on the walk along the lake, and a little blustery too. I didn't care. I had Kevin now, so I felt as toasty as a caterpillar in its cocoon.

"So," I said as we looked out at the city. "There's one thing that's different since we last talked. I've gotten into screenwriting."

"Yeah?" Kevin said. "I can see you doing that."

"And I have this screenwriter friend—she was nominated for an Oscar once."

"Cool."

"But she thinks I need to move to Los Angeles."

"Yeah?"

"Yeah."

Kevin thought for a second, staring out through the metal webbing that they put up to keep people from jumping off and committing suicide. In front of us were the finished skyscrapers of downtown. To our left was the South Lake Union area—where most of the new buildings were rising, almost all of them still unfinished. Some of them were just cranes and scaffolding or even open pits. Amazon hadn't even started building its big geodesic balls.

"Okay," he said at last. "Let's go. You mean, like, this summer?"

"Wait," I said. "Go back. Are you saying you want to come with me?"

"Um, hello? Just picked you over Colin, remember? Besides, I think it's time for a change."

"But..."

"What?"

"Well, how can you be sure you and I will still be together this summer? How do you know for sure you'll even want to live with me?"

He half shrugged and kept staring out at the city. "I just know."

"Kevin."

He turned to me. "What?" he said. Before I said that Kevin's smile was inscrutable, beyond even Leonardo da Vinci's understanding. But it wasn't that way now. On the contrary, he looked completely sincere, completely open. It was sort of freaking me out.

"*How* can you know?" I said. He and I had had this conversation once back in high school—about how the future was impossible to predict, and that you couldn't ever truly *know* you were going to be in love with someone in a month or a year (and that maybe that was okay).

Kevin kept smiling, his hair blowing a little in the wind. Out beyond the webbing, a thousand glittery eyes watched us with bated breath—all the lights of the city.

"Russel, it's all good," he said. "After everything we've been through? We're meant to be together. It's the most obvious thing in the world. Can't you see that?"

It *was* obvious. But now I wasn't the only one thinking it. Now Kevin was too. And maybe that meant it wasn't just an illusion. Maybe that meant it was finally real.

"We're really going to do this?" I said. "We're really going to live together? And we're really going to move to Los Angeles?"

"We really are," he said.

And to prove that I really might make it as a screenwriter one day, I think this just might be the perfect place to fade to black.

The story continues in:
Barefoot in the City of Broken Dreams,
about Russel and Kevin's adventures in Los Angeles

ALSO BY BRENT HARTINGER

ABOUT THE AUTHOR

Brent Hartinger is an author and screenwriter. *Geography Club*, the book in which Russel Middlebrook first appears (as a teenager), is also a successful stage play and a feature film co-starring Scott Bakula. It's now being adapted as a television series.

Brent's other books include the gay teen mystery/thriller *Three Truths and a Lie*, which was nominated for an Edgar Award.

As a screenwriter, Brent currently has four film projects in development.

In 1990, Brent helped found the world's third LGBT teen support group, in his hometown of Tacoma, Washington. In 2005, he co-founded the entertainment website AfterElton.com, which was sold to MTV/Via-com in 2006. He currently co-hosts a podcast called Media Carnivores from his home in Seattle, where he lives with his husband, writer Michael Jensen. Read more by and about Brent, or contact him at brenthartinger.com.

ACKNOWLEDGEMENTS

As usual, I couldn't do any of this alone. It all begins with my partner and husband Michael Jensen; my agent Jennifer De Chiara; and my editor Stephen Fraser. Talk about your holy trinities.

The amazing (and amazingly patient) Philip Malaczewski did my book jacket. The sublime Brett Every kindly volunteered his time and talent to write a song based on this book, and Jeremy Ward helped create the accompanying music video that I hope you'll check out. The eagle-eyed Amanda Coffin was my copy editor (though any remaining errors are entirely *my* fault).

Early readers who generously contributed their time and extremely helpful opinions include Connor Allison, Gervan Ameaud, Brian Centrone, Bill Konigsburg, Steve Leonard, Peter Monn, Tim O'Leary, Jesse Parks, Mike Querez, and Robin Reardon.

And my life as an artist would be far more difficult without the advice and constant support of my assortment of creative genius friends: Tom Baer, Tim Cathersal, Lori Grant, Erik Hanberg, Marcy Rodenborn, James Venturini, and Sarah Warn.

70430184R00156